BRIDE OR DIE

LAURA DURHAM

BROADMOOR BOOKS

CHAPTER 1

"What do you mean the groom's father thinks you're aliens?" I asked, pressing my phone to my ear as I paced in front of the stone church.

Even though it was July in Washington, DC, the day was slightly overcast, and I peered up at the slate-gray clouds moving slowly overhead. I knew I should be grateful that it wasn't sweltering, since summer in the city was usually a sticky affair, but between the impending rainstorm and MIA father of the groom, I wasn't feeling very lucky.

"Did I mention that he's dressed like he stepped off the set of *Men in Black*, and he won't take off his sunglasses?" my assistant, Kate, asked me from the other end of the phone.

I rubbed the wrinkles that were quickly forming between my eyes. As the owner of Wedding Belles, one of the city's most successful wedding planning firms, I was used to brides being jittery, mothers being high-strung, and grooms being nervous. I was not used to fathers thinking my leggy, blonde assistant was an alien.

I'd left her at the hotel to load the father into our last limo when he hadn't managed to make it down for the first round of transportation. Typically, Kate was the perfect choice to sweet-talk fathers, grandfathers, or groomsmen. She knew just how much to flutter her eyelashes and had no problem laughing at some bad dad jokes.

"Does this mean he won't be joining us for the ceremony?" I asked, wondering if I even wanted to deal with a delusional dad at this point. Getting the bride down the aisle on time was priority number one, and we were already in danger of running late.

"He wants to talk to one of his sons," Kate said in a low voice.

I looked over my shoulder at the arched wooden doors that dominated the front of the church. As if I'd willed him to appear, Fern, my go-to wedding hairdresser, popped his head out of one side. His dark hair was pulled into a pristine pony-tail at the nape of his neck, and a giant topaz ring glittered on his hand that gripped the door.

"Annabelle," he said. "The humidity is wreaking havoc on the bride's hair. Are we almost ready to start?"

I waved him over to me, and he hurried out of the church, smoothing his robin's egg blue jacket as he walked. True to form, Fern had matched his attire to the wedding colors, and for a moment I wondered if he'd had a jacket made from the same fabric as the bridesmaids' gowns before realizing that would be over-the-top, even for him.

"The groomsmen are still lined up at the back of the church, right?" I asked when he reached me.

"Just where you left them." He gave me a small smirk. "Luckily, most of them are bald so humidity isn't an issue on that side of the aisle."

"I need one of the groom's brothers," I told him. "It's kind of an emergency. Would you mind sending one out here?"

He spun on his heel, and I noticed that his shoes *did* have a chunky heel almost as high as mine. "You got it, sweetie." He paused halfway back up the stone steps to the church and looked over his shoulder. "Which ones are the groom's brothers?"

"The only two with hair."

He gave me a thumbs-up, and slipped back into the church, reappearing moments later with a tall blond in a classic tuxedo. "Will this one do?" Fern asked, arching an eyebrow and giving the groomsman an obvious once-over.

The man looked from me to Fern and back again, his confusion evident.

"Sorry," I said, walking toward him. "We have a little issue we thought you might be able to help us out with."

"Dad?" He asked with a sigh.

"Actually, yes. He doesn't seem to want to get in the limo we have for him." I hesitated. "He thinks my assistant and the limo drivers are aliens trying to abduct him."

The man rolled his eyes as Fern's jaw went slack behind him. The groomsman held out his hand. "I'll talk to him."

"Kate," I said into my phone. "I've got one of the groom's brothers."

I passed the phone over and stepped aside to give the guy some privacy. Fern sidled up to me. "It was only a matter of time, you know."

"For what?" I whispered.

"I always thought my first alien abductee would be a bride," Fern mused, tapping a finger on his chin. "An older father of the groom is an odd choice."

"He was not abducted by aliens," I said under my breath.

"Then why is he so scared of them?" Fern gave me a knowing look. "The poor dear must have had a horrible time of it when he was taken."

I put a hand to my temples and rubbed. "Please don't tell me you believe alien abductions are real."

Fern gaped at me. "You don't?" He patted my hand. "I think we can both admit that aliens are clearly walking among us. How else do you explain the Kardashians?"

I closed my eyes for a second and drew in a deep breath, trying to ignore the distinct scent of rain and the fact that the day's wedding was quickly going off the rails. "All I want to do is get through this wedding and recover in time for my own wedding."

"I suppose now is not the time to remind you that Kate and I both warned you off of scheduling your wedding the weekend after a Wedding Belles wedding?"

I opened my eyes and narrowed them immediately at him. "It's not like I had a lot of options. We're pretty booked all summer. At least this way, Reese and I have a week afterward for a honeymoon."

Fern patted my back. "I guess it was tough to find two weeks during the summer when none of us were already booked, although perhaps if you hadn't put off the planning for so long…"

"Is now really the best time to be rehashing all this?" I stole a glance at the groom's brother who was still talking to his father in hushed tones.

"You're right. All's well that ends well." Fern wagged his eyebrows up and down. "I, for one, can't wait to get down to Jamaica. There is a giant fruity cocktail with my name all over it."

I felt my shoulders relax as I thought about sitting on the beach sipping on a brightly colored drink with a paper umbrella poking out of the top. One of the reasons I'd wanted to get married far away from the place where I worked was so it wouldn't feel like another day at the proverbial office. "You and me both."

Fern folded his arms and drummed his fingers as he gave me an arch smile. "Annabelle Archer with a few Rum Runners in her is something I'd like to see."

I winked at him. "As long as that's a type of drink."

Fern pretended to be scandalized as the groom's brother walked back to us, holding out my phone.

"He's on his way," the groomsman said, giving me an apologetic look. "Sorry about that. He's going through what we like to call his Tommy Lee Jones phase."

I didn't ask what that meant, but I was infinitely grateful that the dad was en route, and we would be able to start the ceremony on time. A couple of fat raindrops plopped onto the pavement at my feet, and Fern sucked in air.

"It was not supposed to rain today," he cried, running back toward the church doors. "This suit does not do well when it's wet."

I didn't think the silk bridesmaids' gowns would do well in the rain, either, but I crossed my fingers and looked up at the sky, willing the storm to hold off until we got the bridal party and guests back to the hotel for the reception. Once we were safely inside the ballroom, Mother Nature could do her worst, as far as I was concerned.

My eye caught a vehicle approaching the church, but I let out a disappointed breath when I saw that it wasn't the limo. My mood lifted when the white panel van slowed to a stop, and Kate slid out of the passenger side.

"Do I want to know who you hitched a ride with?" I asked as she teetered toward me in her spike heels, tugging down the hem of her short black dress.

"It's me," the deep rumble of a voice from the driver's side made me jump and squint inside the van.

"Mack," I said with a laugh as I recognized the burly florist with a dark red goatee and pierced eyebrow. "I'm not used to seeing you inside a vehicle."

The man was one half of a floral designing duo that was known as much for the fact that they wore head-to-toe leather and were members of a Christian Harley Davidson motorcycle club as they were for their lush florals.

"One of our drivers called in sick, so I've got the van today." Mack hooked a thumb toward the church. "Plus, we have to transfer some of the flowers to the reception after the ceremony, and they're too big to strap onto the back of my bike."

"That's right," I said. I'd momentarily forgotten that the church had not wanted to keep all of the wedding's flowers. "Well, unless anything else crazy happens, we should be on schedule."

"After being accused of trying to abduct the groom's father and take him into my spaceship, I feel like it can only go uphill for me." Kate jerked a thumb over her shoulder. "The limo should be right behind us, by the way."

"If he thought you could fly a spaceship, the man clearly hasn't seen you drive a car," I said.

Mack stifled a laugh, and Kate made a face at me. "How are we progressing on me getting hazard pay for this job?"

"How about all the wedding cake you can eat and slightly wilted flowers on Saturday nights?" I asked.

She cocked her head at me. "Those are not benefits, Annabelle. Those are leftovers."

"To-may-to, to-mah-to." I put an arm around her shoulders. "So, is this not the best time to tell you that Fern believes aliens walk among us?"

"It would explain a lot of our brides," Kate said.

She wasn't wrong, although I would never admit it out loud.

Mack leaned over the steering wheel and looked up at the sky. "At least this wedding isn't outdoors. You got lucky with that, if nothing else."

"I didn't think it was going to rain today," Kate said, "although, to be honest, I didn't check after Thursday."

"Same here," I admitted, wishing I had more than my standard handful of umbrellas in the trunk of my SUV.

Kate gave me a pointed look. "We can both be forgiven for being a little distracted by *another* wedding."

I glanced over my shoulder as if someone from inside the heavy doors could possibly hear us. My worst nightmare was one of my clients thinking that I'd been distracted by my own wedding planning, although if I was being honest, it would have been impossible not to be distracted. My upcoming wedding to DC police detective Mike Reese seemed to be all any of my friends could talk about.

"I haven't been distracted," I said. "It just got hectic this week."

"Well, don't worry about this." Mack waved a beefy hand at the darkening clouds glowering above us. "According to Doppler, it should pass in an hour, and it isn't at all related to the tropical storm brewing out in the Caribbean."

I stared at him as the words sunk into my brain, then Kate and I both snapped our heads to face each other. "Tropical storm?"

CHAPTER 2

"Well, we did know we were booking the wedding during hurricane season," my fiancé told me the next day, as he handed me one of my chilled, bottled Mocha Frappuccinos from the fridge.

I sat on the kitchen counter in yoga pants and a T-shirt, although we both knew I had no intention of getting anywhere close to a yoga mat. My version of stress relief usually involved baked goods, and I considered running around at a wedding for twelve hours the previous day plenty of exercise.

"But how many hurricanes actually hit the Caribbean in July?" I took a swig of the cold, sweet coffee drink. "Besides, it isn't like we had a ton of options if we wanted to have an engagement that didn't last five years."

Reese swallowed a bite of toast and grinned at me. "Don't look at me. I'm a humble civil servant. You're the business mogul who's booked out eighteen months in advance."

I couldn't help smiling at that. The wedding planning business I'd started from nothing had, indeed, taken off over the past couple of years, and Wedding Belles was in steady demand, despite having raised our prices. Even though it sometimes ran me ragged, my chest swelled with pride at the reminder that being busy was a nice problem to have.

I appraised his broad shoulders, dark hair with its one errant curl that flopped down over his forehead, hazel eyes, and mischievous smile. "I'd hardly call you humble, Detective."

He closed the distance between us, grinning. "You know, I love it when you address me by my proper title."

I laughed and swatted at him, inhaling the subtle spice of his aftershave and feeling a jolt all the way to my toes. "You're impossible." I leveled a finger at him, glancing over my shoulder at the opening between the kitchen and living room. "And don't get any wild ideas. Kate is supposed to be here any minute to work on the last-minute details with me."

Reese cocked his head, wrapping an arm around my waist and nipping at my neck, sending more shivers down my spine. "You mean the details for our hurricane wedding?"

"Stop saying that," I managed to murmur as he kissed his way up my neck, my resolve seriously wavering. "It isn't a hurricane, and I'm sure it isn't going to make landfall in Jamaica. I mean, what are the chances?"

Reese finally reached my lips and gave me a kiss that made me almost melt into a puddle on the Formica counter. When he pulled away, he grinned wickedly and pulled his phone out of his pants pocket. "Do you want to know the actual percentage?"

I rolled my eyes. "Of course not. It will just panic me. Besides, the weather report always changes as the week progresses. You can't count on anything you read a week out."

The door to our apartment flew open and a figure in a yellow rain slicker burst in. A smaller, furrier figure in a matching rain jacket followed behind, scampering around the floor and sniffing at everything.

"Have no fear!" Richard said, pushing back his yellow hood. "I come bearing an emergency evacuation plan."

"Emergency evacuation plan?" Reese muttered, his gaze sweeping our one-bedroom apartment.

Richard gave him a severe look. "If you think I'm going to

be trapped on an island without an evacuation plan, you're out of your mind." He pulled a sheaf of papers out of one of his jacket's patch pockets and waved them in the air. "All I'm missing is a reliable private plane and a bunker."

Reese took a sip of his coffee and nodded. "That sounds reasonable."

Reasonable was not a word I usually associated with my best friend Richard Gerard. As the owner of one of DC's top catering companies—Richard Gerard Catering—he was known for being particular about food quality and unwavering in his attention to detail. That meant that his parties were flawless, and his waitstaff was constantly on the verge of nervous breakdowns.

"What are you wearing?" I tried to ignore my fiancé's smirk and put a hand on my heart as it hammered wildly.

"The proper attire to ride out a hurricane, of course." Richard walked into the kitchen to join us with his tiny Yorkie, Hermès, close on his heels.

I noticed that, despite his attire, Richard's dark, spiky hair was perfectly coiffed, and his skin had a golden glow that could only be obtained from bronzer. Never let it be said that he let hysteria cramp his grooming routine.

Reese glanced down at the dog in the miniature raincoat. "I thought maybe you'd decided to sell your own line of fish sticks."

Richard looked like he wasn't sure whether to scowl or not, as he peered down at his dog. "Hermès would make an excellent product mascot, but can you imagine me promoting anything called a 'fish stick'?"

I couldn't. "I'm assuming all this is to make a point about the potential for bad weather on our wedding day?"

Richard gaped at me, and Hermès yipped. "Bad weather? Sweetie, this is not bad weather. Bad weather was that heat wave that melted the wedding cake at the Meridian House wedding or the ice storm that turned the two hundred person wedding into a one hundred person wedding. This is a hurricane. Houses flying through the air, witches on broomsticks, the whole works."

"I'm pretty sure you're talking about tornados," Reese said over the top of his coffee mug. "And last I checked it was still a tropical storm over the ocean."

Richard fluttered a hand at him, scooping up Hermès and holding him up. "Regardless, little dogs do not fare well in high winds. One strong gust and he'd be gone for good."

I slipped off the kitchen counter and patted Hermès on the head through his rain hood. "I promise you Hermès will not be blown away. It isn't even a hurricane yet. And it has an entire week to peter out or move out to sea."

Richard shook his head. "Since we all fly down on Wednesday, it only has three days to lose intensity. I, for one, am not flying on one of those ridiculous little planes into a storm. They're horrific enough in good weather."

He was still scarred from the prop plane we'd taken on our site visit to Jamaica to select the venue. There had been no flight attendant—a cardinal sin in Richard's eyes—and only a curtain between us and the pilots. The co-pilot peeking back from behind the curtain to yell that we were doing great had not been comforting to Richard, who had white-knuckled the flight and sworn up and down he would never fly commercial again.

"I'm sure they won't fly if the weather is bad," I assured Richard. "And you know those small planes are actually pretty safe."

Richard made a noise in the back of his throat that told me he did *not* agree.

"As much as I'd like to stick around for this," Reese said, bending down to give me a kiss. "I'd better head to work. I still have to put in half a week."

"Don't worry," Richard told him. "I've got this well in hand. You go off and catch some criminals, Detective."

Reese gave me another kiss, this one lingering long enough to make my fingers buzz. "Everything is going to be fine, babe. As long as I'm marrying you, the rest is window dressing."

I smiled up at him, my shoulders instantly relaxing. "Thanks."

I heard Richard let out an impatient huff of breath behind us, but I ignored him as I watched my hot fiancé walk out the door.

"I mean, really," Richard said, once he was gone. "Window dressing? He thinks everything we do is window dressing?"

"He didn't mean it that way." I took my bottled coffee and headed out of the kitchen for the living room. "But you and I both know that a perfect wedding doesn't mean anything about the couple or the marriage. And you know my theory."

Richard followed me, holding Hermès under his arm like a football. "Your inverse wedding budget happiness theorem?"

"The more lavish and over-the-top the wedding, the more chance that the marriage will go up in flames."

Richard stole a look over his shoulder as if we were being listened in on. "First of all, that isn't scientific. Secondly, I would kindly ask you keep that to yourself. If my clients think that bare-bones weddings are the way to go, I'm as good as finished."

I had to admit that my business benefitted from couples wanting elaborate celebrations they could never pull together on their own, so I had no intention of spreading my theory. And Richard was right—it was far from scientific. "You know this isn't something I talk about openly."

"Thank heavens for small favors," he murmured, depositing Hermès on my yellow twill couch.

"Small favors?" Kate asked, as she walked into the apartment carrying a thick binder. "Please tell me this isn't one more thing we have to get down to the island. The favors had better be very small, because there isn't going to be a spare inch in our luggage."

"No." I laughed. "No favors."

"We wouldn't have to worry about luggage limits if you weren't having us each take linen overlays in our bags," Richard said.

Kate's eyes flicked up and down his shiny yellow raincoat, but she didn't comment on it. "If there were decent linens on the island, we wouldn't have to, but you said you refused to sit at a table with bubble gum pink tablecloths."

Richard made a face. "Not unless I'm at a baby shower, and we know that will never happen."

"There we go." Kate dropped her binder on the couch as she kicked off her high-heeled mules. "The hotel's standard linen is pink, so if we want something else, we need to bring it."

Richard shuddered and rubbed his yellow vinyl arms. "In what world is pink the default linen color?"

"The Caribbean," Kate and I both said.

Richard turned to me as I sank into the overstuffed chair across from the couch and tucked my feet up under me. "You know I'm all for drama, darling, but remind me again why we're flying down to Jamaica for your wedding."

I sighed. "You know if I get married here it will be a mess. The venues will be upset if I pick one over the other. The same goes for photographers and bands. This way, I'm not playing favorites, and no one can get their feelings hurt. And since it's a small, destination wedding, they also can't get upset if they aren't invited."

Richard put his hands on his hips. "Speaking of the guest list, how did your mother take the news of a small wedding?"

"She adjusted."

"Did she?" Richard gave me a look that told me he had his doubts. He'd met my mother when she'd shown up out of the blue at my engagement party, and they'd become fast friends, probably because they both had expensive taste and were equally horrified by my more laid-back style. It had been a shock to realize how much my mother and best friend were alike, and way too much to have them together for any length of time.

"A lot of her society friends would rather put bamboo shoots under their fingernails than fly to Jamaica, so I promised that we'd come to Charlottesville and let her throw a reception afterward."

"I'm sure she won't have pink tablecloths at her party," Richard said.

"I'm sure she won't." Knowing my mother, the cloths would be ivory linen and starched to within an inch of their life. Part of me hoped that I could put off her reception for so long that she'd eventually forget about it, although I doubted I could wait her out. I was her only child, after all, and she'd been waiting to throw a wedding since I'd been born. I was just glad she'd taken a backseat role in my actual wedding planning.

Richard sniffed. "So, your mother has to throw a second wedding just so you can keep feathers unruffled with the DC wedding community?"

"Trust me," I said. "She's just thrilled I'm getting married."

"Speaking of feathers being ruffled," Kate said. "Have you talked to Fern lately?"

"You mean since yesterday, when we spent almost the entire day together?"

Kate flopped down on the couch between her binder and Hermès. "So not today then?"

I sat up. "No, why?"

Fern burst through the open door, his eyes scanning the room and fixing on me. "Tell me it isn't true, Annabelle."

CHAPTER 3

"*W*hat isn't true?" I asked as Fern flounced into the room, his familiar scent of high-end hair products wafting over to me, as he sank onto the couch next to Kate and almost on top of Hermès.

Fern flicked his gaze to Kate. "A little bird told me that you're not having a bachelorette party."

I looked at Kate—certain she was the little bird in question—but she wouldn't meet my eyes. "That's right. There's just no time, and you know I'm not into club hopping."

Fern wrinkled his nose. "Who said anything about club hopping, sweetie? That's so déclassé these days, anyway." He brushed nonexistent lint off his Madras plaid blazer. "Bachelorette parties are events unto themselves nowadays—spa weekends, trips to Paris, vineyard crawls."

"Then I definitely don't have time for that. My wedding is this coming weekend, remember?" To be fair to Kate, she had tried to talk me into a bachelorette party weeks ago, but I'd been too overwhelmed with June weddings to think about it. And I was very aware of the trend in over-the-top bachelor and bachelorette parties, although I found myself nostalgic for the days where things were simpler. Between jet-setting bachelor parties and Instagram-worthy promposals, it seemed like overkill was now par for the course.

"Of course, I remember," Fern said. "I'm doing everyone's hair. That doesn't mean we can't slip in a little celebration once we're on the island."

Kate's eyes brightened. "I could research sunset booze cruises."

"This entire discussion is pointless." Richard folded his arms over his chest and his shiny raincoat made a strange squelching sound.

Fern glanced at him and frowned, as if he was just now noticing Richard's odd outfit in light of the hot DC weather. "Spoilsports don't have to attend."

Richard sighed. "It's not that I don't relish attending an event with the word 'booze' in its name, but we aren't going to be flying down to the Caribbean at all."

Fern glanced from me to Richard and back again. "Why? Is the wedding off? Did that gorgeous scamp with muscles for miles run out on you?"

"Of course not," I said, glad that Reese wasn't present to hear himself described as a scamp. "Richard is convinced that weather will make us cancel."

"Weather?" Fern pulled out his phone. "I haven't even peeked at the weather down in the Caribbean. Isn't it usually sweltering and humid in July?" He glanced up at me. "Don't worry sweetie. I'm packing lots of setting spray, so your hair won't wilt."

"There's a little tropical storm in the Caribbean," Kate said, "but it's not an issue."

Richard muttered about Kate's concept of size being surprising considering all the men she dated, and she shot him a look.

As Fern tapped away on his phone, I took a final swig of my cold coffee as my own phone vibrated on the end table next to me. Grabbing it, I peered down at the screen and saw a familiar number pop up on the screen. "That's odd."

"What?" Kate jerked her head toward me. "It isn't the bride from yesterday, is it? Her mom? The groom?"

Like me, Kate dreaded calls from anyone in the wedding party the day after. It usually meant someone had lost something or left something at the wedding venue. That meant they wanted us to place emergency calls to vendors or even personally search for the errant phone or purse or shoes. Luckily, we hadn't gathered up any abandoned items at the end of the night and the number wasn't connected to yesterday's wedding.

"It's Amanda," I told her, still staring at the name on the screen.

"You mean our old bride Amanda?" Kate tilted her head at me. "Why would she be calling? Her wedding was almost six months ago. Doesn't she know that we broke up with her?"

I tried to give my assistant a severe look, but it devolved into a grin. Kate liked to joke that we broke up with our brides as soon as we left their wedding reception for the night, although both of us knew it rarely worked out that way. Her reasoning was that our contract was over, the service was delivered, and we needed to move on. Brides did not see it that way.

I was fine with easing clients off, and I always expected a few days of wrap-up calls and emails. Six months did seem like a stretch.

"Let me see what she wants." I stood up and headed down the hall to my home office, Kate's warnings not to answer following me until I closed the door to the small office. I pushed to answer the call, as I sat down in the black office chair. "Wedding Belles. This is Annabelle."

"Annabelle. I'm so relieved you picked up." The bride's voice was much as I remembered it—direct and efficient, although with an unfamiliar twinge of panic that seemed very out of character.

"Hi, Amanda. It's nice to hear from you after so long."

She let out a breath. "I know it must be odd for me to call you up out of the blue."

"Not at all. Are you having an issue with one of your wedding vendors?"

It wasn't unusual for issues to pop up with wedding vendors months later. Usually it involved videos running late or photo albums delayed, but Amanda Hart had hired all top-tier vendors, so I would have been a little surprised if that had been the case. Everything about the Hart-McCoy wedding had been top-tier, including the beauty pageant bride and the political TV pundit groom.

"Nothing like that," Amanda said. "I thought you might be able to help me with something else."

"Okay." I was starting to regret not taking Kate's advice and answering the call. "You do know we exclusively plan weddings."

"It's not about event planning. I need your crime-solving skills."

I didn't answer for a moment. It wasn't surprising that she'd heard about our occasional run-ins with a dead body—especially since some of our rivals had made sure to spread the word—but I'd hoped that our stretch of several months without one would have helped the gossip die down. Apparently not.

I took a deep breath to steady myself. "Crime solving isn't something we actively pursue. Yes, we've had some bad luck, but I don't want you to think— "

"Annabelle, please." Amanda cut me off. "My husband is missing."

My mind went quickly to her groom. I didn't watch a lot of TV, and I definitely avoided the political shows, but Brock McCoy was a well-known media personality and political pundit, with his own show where he skewered both sides of the aisle. Well-known enough for even me to recognize him on sight when we'd met.

Tall and classically handsome, he also possessed whatever charisma made the camera love him and people feel drawn to him. He was striking enough to attract stares and charming enough to make most women swoon. Like most people in the public eye, he'd been somewhat guarded. I hadn't gotten to know him well during the planning, but he'd never been difficult or demanding.

"What do you mean he's missing?"

Amanda choked back a sob. "He went on his run early this morning, as usual. But when he didn't come back and jump in the shower, I started to worry. That's usually how I wake up. I hear him in the shower and roll out of bed. But he never came home, and I overslept. When I finally went downstairs, there was no sign of him."

I tried to keep the impatience out of my voice. "Don't you think it's possible he went for a longer run than usual?"

"He would never miss his show. I had to call the station and tell them he was sick to cover for him, but I know something is wrong."

"Then you should call the police," I said.

"They won't do anything since he's only technically been missing for a few hours. They'll think he left me."

"Not necessarily," I said. "Why would they think he would run out on you?"

Now she sighed deeply. "We've been having some ups and downs lately. The last thing either of us needs is to have a scandal, but I have a really bad feeling about this."

"Amanda, I'm a wedding planner, not a detective. You really need to call the — "

"I can't. Not yet. It will make it all feel too real. I just need someone to help me look at things clearly, and you were always so good at that during my wedding planning." She hitched in a breath. "You were the only one who could calm me down and make me look at things rationally. You know my sister and best friend will be useless."

I did remember her bridal party. Like her, they'd all been pageant girls, but none of them were quite as sharp and successful as Amanda had been, and I would have never used the word rational to describe any of them.

I bit my bottom lip. My gut was telling me to hang up and change my cell phone number. But Amanda had never been a bridezilla. Even though she'd had moments of bridal stress, and I'd had to talk her out of walking down a giant mirror aisle, she had never been hysterical or prone to exaggeration. If she thought her husband was missing, I tended to believe her.

Of course, I knew it wasn't my job to help her through this, but something—maybe the desperation in her voice or my own desire to be distracted from my wedding week drama—made me want to help her.

"Is there any way you could pop over today?" she asked. "If you think I'm crazy after I tell you everything, I promise I won't bother you again."

Before I could think too hard about it I answered. "Okay, but I'm probably going to tell you to call the police."

"I knew I could count on you, Annabelle. There's a reason you're the best wedding planner in the city."

"Yeah, yeah," I mumbled as I hung up, immediately regretting my decision because I knew I'd have to tell Kate. And Richard. I groaned. Richard was going to kill me. He already accused me of attracting criminal investigations when I stumbled into them. I knew he would consider this running headlong into one.

Squaring my shoulders and preparing for a major argument, I walked back out to the living room. Kate was rubbing Fern's back as he appeared to hyperventilate into a paper bag while Richard paced back and forth with his phone pressed to his ear. They hadn't overheard my conversation, had they?

"What's going on?"

Kate waved her phone in the air as Fern let out a muffled wail. "That tropical storm has strengthened into a category 4 hurricane and it's headed straight for Jamaica. I just got a call from the resort saying they're going to have to board everything up."

"Hurricane Dolly," Fern said, his voice muffled by the paper bag. "Now my favorite Broadway show is ruined forever."

Richard held his hand over his phone. "Far be it from me to say I told you so, darling."

A knot formed in the pit of my stomach. After all this, was I going to have to cancel my wedding?

CHAPTER 4

I flopped down onto the couch as the disappointment washed over me. After all the weddings I'd successfully steered away from disaster, was my own wedding going to fall apart at the last minute?

Leaning my head back and staring up at the ceiling, I blinked away tears. Fern's heaving breaths into the paper bag stopped, as did Richard's pacing.

"Is she crying?" Fern said in a stage whisper, as if he wasn't sitting next to me.

"I don't know," Kate whispered back.

I sat up and swiped at my eyes with the back of my hand. "I'm not crying."

My friends gaped at me, including Richard who held his phone away from his mouth and seemed frozen in mid-pace.

Seeing them all so concerned made tears prick the backs of my eyelids again, and I let out an exasperated sigh. "Maybe I am crying. Can't I get upset sometimes?"

"But you never lose it," Kate said. "You're the only one of us who doesn't, no matter what happens."

I put the heels of my palms over my eyes so I wouldn't have to see their worried expressions, and so the tears wouldn't flow freely down my cheeks. "Just because I seem calm, doesn't mean I don't get upset. I know it seems like I haven't been excited about wedding planning, but I am excited about marrying Reese." I heaved in a breath. "And now that may not happen."

"Well, if you're going to cry, then you know I'm going to cry," Fern said, his hyperventilating quickly morphing into sniffles. "Never let it be said that Fern let a woman cry alone."

"It's going to be okay, Annie." Kate put a hand on my arm as Fern's sniffles became sobs.

I opened my eyes, and a tear rolled down my cheek. "Thanks, but it's really not. Even I can't fix a hurricane."

"Hurricane or not," Richard said, flinging off his raincoat and tossing it over one of my dining room chairs, "You are going to have a fabulous wedding on Saturday."

I glanced back at him. "That's less than a week away, and we don't have a venue. Everything we spent so long putting together for my wedding in Jamaica is out the window."

Richard flicked his hand as if brushing away my concern. "Then we start over. I've planned events in less than a week."

"You've planned a wedding from start to finish in less than a week?" Kate asked.

Richard ignored her question as he strode over to stand in front of us. Hermès jumped down from his spot and scampered in circles around Richard's legs. "As God is my witness, Annabelle, you will get married on Saturday and it will be spectacular."

Fern looked up from his weeping. "Where's your carrot, Scarlett?"

Richard slapped his leg. "I can't do this alone, and I won't have my staff crying on company time."

Fern blinked hard. "Staff? Since when am I your—?"

"Since I took charge of this emergency wedding planning," Richard said, spinning on his heel and pacing again. "Time is of the essence, so we're going to need to divide and conquer.

Obviously, I'll take the hard part—locating an available venue on short notice—but I need everyone pitching in."

I'd seen plenty of Richard's bossy side, but never had I seen him rally the troops quite so militantly. "You really think you can do it, and it will be nice? I don't want a wedding in a rec center."

Richard swiveled around and gave me a withering look. "Do I look like I've ever set foot in a rec center?" He made a face like he'd smelled sour milk. "Honestly, Annabelle. Would I plan anything that wasn't impeccable?"

I held up my hands. "You're right. My bad."

He inclined his head slightly. "You're forgiven, darling. You are the bride, after all." He narrowed his eyes at Kate and Fern. "The rest of you have no such excuse."

Fern shrunk back, his hand pressed against his heart. "I don't know whether to be terrified or turned on."

"Terrified," Kate mumbled quietly. "With Richard, always terrified."

I smiled at my best friend, a lump welling up in my throat. I should have known that Richard would not let my wedding be ruined. He might be finicky and bossy, but he was also a loyal friend. I also knew he did not want to lose his opportunity to be both my Man of Honor and one of Reese's groomsmen. I didn't know how he'd managed to finagle himself onto both sides of the wedding party, but he'd done it, and I suspected my wedding was almost as important to him as it was to me.

"Thanks, Richard," I said, my voice cracking.

"Don't mention it, darling." He gave me a brief, warm smile before going back to tapping a finger to his chin. "We already have Buster and Mack doing decor, but they'll need to have flowers sent here instead of Jamaica, and the tropicals they'd been planning to use may not work here."

"Why not?" Kate asked. "I think a planner with your talent should be able to replicate the look of a Caribbean wedding in DC."

Richard considered her for a moment, arching his perfect brows. "You're right, of course. The look doesn't have to change. If we can't go to Jamaica, we'll bring Jamaica to us — depending on the venue, of course. You know how I hate a mis-match." He pointed at Kate. "You're in charge of working with Buster and Mack to make sure that happens plus coordinating rental linens and china now that we're local."

Kate clapped her hands. "Yes! No more pink tablecloths."

Fern scooted to the edge of the sofa. "What about me?"

Richard leveled a finger at him. "I need you to use your considerable contacts to find us an officiant and get Annabelle's marriage license. The last thing she needs is to go down to the DC courthouse."

Fern straightened his shoulders. "I'm on it. I love the courthouse!"

I turned to look at him in disbelief. "You love the DC courthouse?"

Fern shrugged. "The plastic flower gazebo in the marriage bureau? It's so kitsch, it's chic."

I wasn't sure I agreed, but I was grateful I wouldn't have to do it. "So, venue, decor, marriage license and officiant. What else do we need?"

"It goes without saying that Richard Gerard Catering will handle all food and beverage," Richard said. "But we will need entertainment."

"By this point all the good dance bands will be booked," Kate said. "Let's hope all the steel drummers aren't taken."

Richard wrinkled his nose. "Are we really going to be expected to dance to steel drummers?"

"Do you dance?" Kate asked him, folding her arms over her chest and eyeing him.

"Of course, I do. I'm an excellent dancer."

I leaned into Kate. "He and PJ danced at Leatrice's wedding, remember?"

"Speaking of your significant other…" Kate began, her grin

widening.

Richard flicked his gaze to her. "We are dividing wedding tasks, young lady, not discussing my personal life."

"Yoo hoo!"

We all looked up as a jet-black poof of hair appeared in my doorway. I knew I shouldn't be surprised. My downstairs neighbor, Leatrice, had an uncanny ability to know when I had company. Even though she was over eighty, I was convinced she had incredibly good hearing. Reese was equally convinced she had us under some sort of illegal surveillance. Considering her fondness for espionage—and her tendency to believe most people in DC were foreign agents, as well as her habit of wearing disguises and following them—Reese was probably right.

"Leatrice," Richard said, more of a curse than a greeting.

"I thought I heard you kids up here," she said as she stepped inside. "It sounds like a party."

It looked like Leatrice had started to get into the island spirit early. She wore a garish floral print halter top that showed a scary amount of wrinkled skin over a matching skirt and had tucked a hot pink silk flower into her jet-black Mary Tyler Moore flip hairdo. It was a testament to how conditioned we all were to Leatrice's creative clothing that none of us blinked twice.

"Only if you consider emergency wedding planning a party," Kate said.

Her painted-on eyebrows shot skyward. "What's the emergency? Pregnant bride? Groom headed to prison?"

"If you must know," Richard said, his tone already exaggerated. "We need to pull together a wedding for Annabelle since a hurricane is headed for Jamaica and the hotel is shutting down."

Her bright coral lips formed a perfect "O" to match her wide eyes. "The wedding on the island is off?"

"I'm afraid so," I said. "But Richard promises that he can

pull one together here that will be just as wonderful."

Leatrice pulled herself up to her full height, which still meant she was pushing five feet. "Then you can count on my Sidney Allen for entertainment."

Kate and I exchanged a glance. Leatrice had recently married the dramatic, pint-sized entertainment coordinator she'd met at one of my weddings. Their romance had been a shock to us all because Sidney Allen wasn't what I'd ever thought of as leading man material—and I'd never heard of him dating. But one thing I'd learned over years of wedding planning was that the course of love was not something I could ever predict. And that there truly was someone for everyone, no matter how quirky.

And Sidney Allen was quirky. Shaped somewhat like Humpty Dumpty, he coordinated his entertainment with wireless headsets and code names for all of his performers. He was known primarily for his costumed performers, and he'd provided scores of masked Venetian characters straight out of Carnival for one of our weddings and a full Cirque du Soleil performance for another.

"Don't you and your husband want to enjoy the wedding as guests?" I asked, trying to diplomatically extricate myself from having Sidney Allen storm around my wedding screaming into his headset.

Leatrice waved a bony hand at me. "You know my Honeybun. He's happiest when he's running the show—literally. Besides, you need entertainment, don't you?"

I hesitated. We did, and I knew none of us had time to sift through options. From Richard's deep sigh, he knew it, too.

"Fine," Richard said, pointing at her. "But tell Honeybun to keep it on theme and understated."

Leatrice gave him a sharp salute. "You can count on us, General Gerard."

Richard shook his head and cast his eyes heavenward. "Give me strength."

CHAPTER 5

"*A*re you going to tell me where we're going, Annabelle?" Kate asked once we were sitting safely in my car. "I know Richard can be a little intense, but I don't know if turning into a runaway bride is the answer."

I gave her a withering look. "I'm not pulling a runner, but I do need a breather. Between the hurricane and Richard turning my apartment into his new emergency wedding re-planning headquarters, it's all a little much."

"So, are we going to stuff our faces with cupcakes from Baked and Wired or eat an entire bag of chocolate croissants from Patisserie Poupon?" She rubbed her hands together. "Or both?"

I glanced down the narrow Georgetown street in front of my stone-fronted apartment building, peering up at my fourth floor windows. I hated to give up such a prime parking spot on P Street, but I also *had* to get out of there. "We're going to Amanda and Brock's place."

Kate twisted around in the passenger seat, sliding her sunglasses down her nose to peer at me. "That sounds way less fun than cupcakes or chocolate croissants. Amanda and Brock as in The Mellon Auditorium and gold and lilac?"

I nodded as I started my SUV and eased it out of the space. Kate liked to remember couples by their venues and their colors. I usually remembered them by their crazy family members. "Yep. Drunk great aunt who kept hitting on the groomsmen."

Kate grinned, snapping her fingers. "Oh, yeah. I loved her."

I didn't say that I wasn't surprised. The great aunt with the frosted blond hair and inappropriately short dress made me think of what Kate might be like in fifty years.

I rolled down the car windows to let out some of the accumulated heat, but the air outside was as hot as the air inside. Typical Washington DC in July, I thought as I sucked in a stifling breath.

"So, I'm guessing this has to do with the phone call you got from her," Kate said. "You never told me what she wanted. Please don't tell me their marriage blew up, and she's already engaged to someone new. I don't think I can do a repeat client so soon." She put a hand to her heart. "I need time to grieve."

"No grieving required." At least I hoped not. "But it does have something to do with Brock. He's missing."

Kate fanned her face with one hand. "As in really missing or just went on a bender and isn't back yet?"

I frowned at her and hung a right at the stop sign. "Does Brock McCoy strike you as the type of guy to go on a bender?"

Kate thought about it for a moment. "If I'm being honest, no."

"Exactly. Amanda said he never came back from his early morning run, and even missed his show."

"Okay. I'll admit that's strange. I don't watch political shows, but even I know his show is pretty popular. He'd have to be crazy to do something to risk that. But what does any of that have to do with us? Didn't you explain to her that we were broken up?"

I drove toward Wisconsin Avenue, turning on the car's air-conditioning and rolling up the windows. "I tried to explain that missing persons weren't our thing, but she said she heard that we'd solved crimes before."

Kate muttered a string of creative curses under her breath that would have made our Christian biker florist friends blush. "I knew we should have shelled out the big bucks to have a company scrub our social media mentions."

"You know there's no such thing as removing everything from the internet. Besides, it's not like it was just one murder."

"Or kidnapping or jewel heist," she added. "Say what you want, I blame this all on Brianna."

Our number one wedding planning rival was Brianna, owner of Brides by Brianna, a perky blonde who loved nothing more than trying to drag our names through the mud. To be fair, we'd done a fair amount of mud dragging, as well. To be more precise, Fern had, by spreading the rumor that her business was really a front for a call girl service. She'd retaliated by making sure that the hashtag #weddingplannersofdeath trended every time our names were mentioned online.

"We can't blame her for all of it," I said, adjusting the AC vents on my side of the car to point directly at my face. "And we have helped solve all the cases we've been mixed up in. Maybe she's impressed by our 100 percent success rate."

"You're really working to find that silver lining, aren't you, boss?"

I ignored her. "I told her that she should call the police, but she begged me to stop by and help her calm down."

"Well, you are good at calming down hysterical women," Kate said. "And Richard."

"I promise we'll pop in and make sure she's okay and then go. If it's anything more than that we can call Reese."

She cut her eyes to me. "When have I heard this before? You know if Richard finds out what we're doing, a category 4 hurricane will be the least of your worries."

"He won't find out because there's nothing worth mentioning. Brock may be home already by the time we get there." I glanced at the clock in my dashboard. "It has been a couple of hours since she called."

Kate started to mutter something about the best laid plans, but I cut her off before she could mangle the expression. "Do you remember much about him?"

She shrugged. "I remember he's hot, but I also don't remember him being involved in the planning. Did he even come to the tasting?"

I drummed my fingers on the steering wheel as I waited for the light to change. "I think he came late from the TV studio."

"Right," Kate said as if she was slowly retrieving the memory back. "Nikki texted us, didn't she?"

The light turned green, and I drove across Wisconsin Avenue. "I'd forgotten that."

One of our wedding makeup artists also did the makeup for one of the DC affiliate TV stations. Our groom had apparently been chatting with her about having to rush out to his wedding tasting while he'd been in the makeup chair, and she'd texted us when he was on his way, guessing correctly that he might forget to.

"Aside from knowing that he has great hair, a perfect smile, and camera-ready groomsmen," Kate said. "I honestly couldn't tell you much more about him. I don't even know which side of the aisle he's on."

"Both and neither," I told her. "He's known for being equally tough on both parties on his political round-up show. I honestly think he's made enemies on both sides."

"What's the angle on that? I thought most pundits went all in on a side in hopes of getting a job in a partisan think tank or super PAC."

I would have been surprised that Kate was so well-versed on political pundits, think tanks, and super PACs, but I remembered that she'd dated men who worked in all three.

That was before she'd sworn off dating men in politics and had gotten closer to my fiancé's brother, Daniel. Lately, she'd been uncharacteristically close-lipped about her dating life.

"I think Brock wants to stick to television broadcasting," I said, recalling hearing Amanda talk about her husband-to-be's career as she'd gotten ready for the wedding. "I don't think he wants to parlay his show into anything but a bigger show with more national appeal on one of the cable stations."

I slowed when I recognized the street the bride and groom lived on — a narrow Georgetown lane lined with historic row houses and shaded by some large trees. Scouring the right side, I braked the car when I recognized their pale yellow house with black shutters.

"And someone's pulling out right in front." Kate waved a finger at a red Saab merging into the street.

Thanking the parking gods, I did a quick reverse to parallel park into the snug space, barely touching the bumper behind me.

"That's not hitting," Kate said, fluttering a hand at me. "It's the city. It's not considered hitting unless you see the car behind you move. That car didn't flinch."

I hopped out of the car, peeked at the other car, saw no scratches and let out a breath. I wasn't sure that *was* the rule, but I was going to go with it for now.

My phone trilled in my purse, and I dug it out as Kate joined me on the sidewalk in front of the house.

"If that's Richard, don't answer it."

"It's not Richard. It's Reese." I slapped my forehead. "I forgot to tell him about the hurricane and Richard and everything."

"You think Richard called and told him? He was pretty immersed in calling venues when we left."

I groaned as my fiancé's number flashed on the phone screen. "No. I think he's at our apartment. He was supposed to come home for lunch." I answered and held the phone to my ear, trying to sound cheery. "Hey, babe, what's up?"

I heard Richard and Fern sniping at each other in the background, Hermès yipping, and what sounded like Leatrice singing an off-key Broadway tune.

My fiancé let out a tortured sigh. "Why don't you tell me?"

CHAPTER 6

"He'll forgive you," Kate patted my arm as we knocked on the shiny black door.

I knew my ever-patient fiancé would forgive me, but I could still kick myself for forgetting to let him know that our entire wedding had changed. Not that there was anything either of us could do about a hurricane, but I did feel a stab of guilt that he had to get the news from an excitable Richard and not me.

"Am I the worst fiancée ever?" I asked in a whisper.

Kate looked shocked by my question. "No way. You're not a great bride, but I think you're a wonderful fiancée."

Now I gaped at her. "How am I not a great bride?" Had I become one of the bridezillas we hated and not even known it?

Kate's expression immediately softened. "I don't mean it like that. I mean that you haven't been into your wedding like other brides are. You know you took forever to settle on a date and a venue. It's taken longer to plan your wedding than it might have if you were focused on the planning."

This was something Kate—and Richard—had accused me of before. In my defense, it was hard to get excited about your own wedding when you planned weddings every day of your life. Before I could remind Kate that my lack of excitement about wedding planning did *not* mean I was a bad bride, the door swung open.

The Amanda I remembered from her wedding—tall and curvy with glossy black hair that framed her face in perfect bouncy waves—looked dramatically different. Her hair was pulled up in a messy ponytail, and she didn't wear a drop of makeup. Her cheeks were pale and her lips bloodless. Even her yoga pants and oversized T-shirt looked grungy. I knew Kate was as startled by her appearance as I was, because neither of us spoke for a few seconds as we took her in.

"Annabelle! Kate!" Her shoulders sagged as her red-rimmed gaze moved between us. "You're here." She hitched in a breath. "You don't know how much it means to me that you came."

"Of course, we came," I said, recovering my voice as she waved us inside.

We followed her down the short entryway, and Kate made wide eyes at me. I nodded at her because I knew what she meant. In the almost year we'd spent working with Amanda on her wedding, we hadn't seen the former Miss Ohio in anything less than designer clothes and a full face of flawless makeup. We'd also never seen a chink in her pageant-perfect persona. This, more than anything, made me think something was genuinely wrong—or at least she was convinced there was.

"I'm sorry for the mess," Amanda said, leading us into the living room and picking up some stray newspapers scattered on the beige couch.

The renovated Georgetown townhouse was much as I remembered it from wedding planning, chic and simple with lots of beige and cream accented with pops of teal and navy. The only noticeable change was the addition of framed wedding portraits on the fireplace mantle and the high narrow table that stretched behind the couch. I glanced at the beaming couple cheek-to-cheek in the photos, memories of the day flashing back to me.

A clattering sound made me look through the open-plan dining room toward the doorway leading to the kitchen. "Did Brock come back?" I asked, not sure whether I should be irritated she didn't cancel our visit or pleased he was okay.

"Is that the wedding planner?" The female voice calling out from the kitchen answered my own question and soon a blonde head of hair poked through the kitchen doorway.

"Your sister is here," Kate said as two women bustled out toward us. "And one of your bridesmaids."

Amanda cast us a quick desperate glance. "I told them not to come, but they wouldn't listen."

"Hi Ava," I said to the sister as I wracked my brain to remember the name of the bridesmaid. They were both beauties and both former pageant girls, like the bride. Unlike Amanda, they had their hair done, eyelashes applied, and were dressed in summery colors.

"Hey, Taylor," Kate said to the brunette of the two, saving me from fumbling for the name.

I gave my assistant a grateful glance. Sometimes Kate really saved my bacon.

"Coffee?" Ava asked, holding out two steaming mugs.

I'd already had my morning quota of caffeine, but I didn't want to be rude, so I took the mug, as did Kate.

"So why are you here again?" Taylor asked, sitting down on one of the chairs angled across from the sofa.

Amanda shot her friend a look, and I instantly remembered Taylor from the wedding. The past Miss Maine was more petite than the other women and had been less than thrilled with the bride's choice of bridesmaids' dress because she'd thought it hadn't flattered her figure. That was the problem with an entire wedding party of pageant beauties. They forgot that a wedding was only allowed one diva.

I gave her my best patient wedding planner smile. "Moral support."

Taylor wrinkled her nose, clearly of the opinion that it was odd for Amanda's wedding planner and assistant to be offering moral support. I didn't totally disagree.

"Annabelle and Kate aren't just wedding planners." Amanda motioned for us to sit on the couch. "They've been known to solve crimes for their clients."

Both Ava's and Taylor's perfectly arched eyebrows shot up. The way she phrased it sounded like it was an add-on service to our wedding planning package, not that Kate hadn't suggested it before.

"Not professionally," I said. "We leave the real work to the police."

Kate made a choked noise behind her coffee mug, which I took great pains to ignore.

The bride's sister's eyes widened, and she touched a hand to her bouncy blond hair. "You're here to help Amanda find Brock?"

I wasn't sure if her expression was disbelief or jealousy or something else, but I ignored that, as well. Instead, I turned to Amanda, who'd taken a seat on the other end of the couch. "You still haven't heard anything from him?"

She sniffled and shook her head. "Nothing. I called him a million times and tried to locate him using the Find My Phone app, but his phone must be turned off."

"And he always takes his phone with him when he runs?"

A hurried nod. "Always. He'd never run without his playlist."

That made sense. "Does he ever normally turn his phone off?"

More head shaking from Amanda. "Not that I've ever known. He has to be reachable by the station. He's never without his phone."

Again, that made sense for just about everyone in DC, especially for someone in the public eye like Brock McCoy.

"How long has it been since he should have returned from his run?" Kate asked.

"Hours." Amanda pulled her knees up onto the couch and rubbed her head. "He missed his show. I ended up sleeping in way later than I usually do, so I didn't notice him gone until way past his call time at the station."

Kate gave me a look before turning back to the bride. "Maybe it's time to call the cops."

A small crease formed between Amanda's eyes. "But then it would get out and there would be a media circus. Brock's been so careful about his career. No scandal. Nothing that could damage his chances to move up in the network."

Kate's blinked rapidly at her. "You think he'll care about that if he's in danger?"

Amanda put a hand over her mouth, then dropped it. "You think he's in danger?"

Kate frowned and looked at me, and it didn't take a mind reader to know what she was thinking. What was Amanda not telling us? The girl looked dazed, but was she seriously out of it?

"If your husband is missing, his phone is off, and there's no reason he'd disappear, then don't you think there's a good chance something is really wrong, and the police need to get involved?" I asked.

Amanda nibbled the corner of her lip. "I was hoping you two could poke around so there didn't have to be any publicity."

Again, with the publicity. I knew she was a pageant queen and he was a TV political pundit, but their public personas couldn't trump safety, could they?

"We don't exactly have the resources of the DC police department," I said, studying Amanda's pinched face. "What are you really worried about if the police get involved?"

She glanced up at her sister and bridesmaid, finally letting out a long breath. "I'm afraid they're going to think that I had a reason for wanting something to happen to Brock."

"You?" Kate and I said at the same time.

I recovered from my surprise first. "You're still newlyweds. Why would you want something to happen to your husband?"

"I wouldn't," Amanda insisted. "But you know how detectives always suspect the spouses first."

From hearing Reese talk about cases, I knew it was rare *not* to include a spouse in an initial suspect list.

"So, you don't want to let the police help you find your missing husband because they might think you're guilty of something you didn't do?" Kate didn't bother to hide the incredulity in her voice.

"It's not just that." Amanda let out a long breath. "If they start asking questions, they're going to find out about the big fight we had in front of our house last night."

The room went quiet.

"How big of a fight?" Ava asked, her voice trembling.

"Big." Amanda dropped her head. "And loud. I'm sure half the neighborhood heard us screaming. Which means they also heard me threaten to kill my husband."

CHAPTER 7

"*I* hate to be the one to say I told you so," Kate said as we drove back to my apartment, my car bumping up and down on the cobbled street.

"I know, I know." I frowned as I stopped at an intersection and looked both ways. "But just because they had a fight and she screamed something awful, doesn't mean she did it."

"Agreed. I don't think she did anything to the guy, but I also don't think we should get involved in what's clearly a personal problem. Even Amanda admitted that her hubby had been acting weird lately and that there's a possibility he just took off."

I glanced over at Kate, who had the window down and her arm propped on the doorframe. "You believe her?"

"Sure." She held up her fingers. "For one, I don't think she'd risk breaking a nail to do anything bad to the guy and two, why call us in and make a big deal about it if she was guilty?"

Kate had a point. Amanda had always struck me as a little ditzy and very preoccupied with her looks, but I would never peg her as a killer—even if she'd threatened to murder her husband.

"What I don't get," Kate continued, "is how hesitant she is

to get the police involved. I mean, she gave us the guy's usual running route. Why not give that to the cops?"

I drummed my fingers on my steering wheel as I accelerated across Wisconsin Avenue. "She and Brock were always very concerned with publicity. Even during the wedding planning. Do you remember how many times they had us rewrite their wedding announcement submission for *The New York Times?*"

"If you ask me, there's a good chance he up and left her and that's why she doesn't want to go to the police. She knows if they dig even a little bit, they'll find that he's shacked up with some other woman."

"What?" I shook my head. "No way. They haven't even been married a year. And I'm with Amanda. Her husband wouldn't risk his TV career for anything."

Kate shrugged. "You'd be surprised what dumb things a guy will do when another woman is involved."

Usually I deferred to Kate's superior knowledge of men, but in this case, I was sure she was wrong.

"Even if I didn't think this was all just some dramatic domestic dispute," Kate said. "We don't have the time to juggle someone's missing husband. Not with an entire wedding to replan."

"Which is why I told Amanda that she should call the police." I made a left, scanning the crowded street for an open parking space.

"You also told her to send you a list of people who might have a reason to harm her husband and took the running route she gave you." Kate twisted to face me. "I hope you don't think we're going to go run the guy's route or something."

I spotted an SUV pulling out of a space and turned on my blinker. "That was just to give her something to do so she wouldn't worry too much."

"Mm hmm." Kate did not sound convinced.

"He is a celebrity of sorts. There's also a chance that he

could have been kidnapped for a ransom. He very well could be tied up somewhere." Even as I said it, I doubted it. If he was being held for a ransom, Amanda would have gotten a call already.

Kate muttered something about there being a greater chance he was tied up by a mistress, but I pretended not to hear her as I angled my car and backed into the parallel street space. I got out of my SUV and joined Kate on the sidewalk, clicking my remote to lock the car.

"You know Richard will pitch a fit if he thinks you're trying to solve a missing persons case during your wedding week," my assistant said, as we walked toward my apartment building.

"Which is why we're not going to tell him that. Primarily, because it isn't true."

Another sound of disbelief from Kate as I opened the heavy wooden door of my building. "I know you hate the idea of saying no to a bride, Annabelle, but if ever there was a time where you were justified, this is it. Besides, her wedding is over. She's not paying us anymore."

"You do remember how well she tipped us, right?"

"With her bridesmaids, we earned every penny of that money."

I couldn't argue with her there. Almost every bridesmaid had been a Miss Something or Other, and each one had been needier than the last. I put my finger to my lips as we stepped inside the small foyer, motioning to the first floor apartment that was home to Leatrice. Although she'd been in my apartment when we left, I did not want to alert her to our return if she'd come downstairs.

We both slipped off our shoes—the only way to pass by Leatrice's door without being heard—and tiptoed up the stairs without speaking. When we reached the fourth floor, we put our shoes back on.

"Promise me." Kate put a hand on my arm as I started to

open the door to my apartment. "We tell Amanda to call the police or handle it on her own."

I met her eyes and saw how serious she was. "Fine. You're right. We don't need any more drama."

I pushed open the door, and we both gaped at the scene before us. Richard was pacing the floor and yelling at someone on the phone while Leatrice and Fern had papers strewn all over the dining table. Hermès—still in his yellow raincoat—was running in fast circles on the coffee table.

"Thank heavens you're back." Richard put his palm over his phone and held it at arm's length.

"What's going on?"

Leatrice beamed at me. "We found an available officiant."

Fern spun on the spot, his arms stretched up over his head. "I can dress as a priest or as my drag persona, Tequila Mockingbird. Not that you need to decide that now, of course."

"I have good news and bad news, Annabelle," Richard said. "Which would you like first?"

"That wasn't the bad news?" Kate mumbled, so only I could hear her.

I rubbed a hand across my forehead. "Worse news than a hurricane hitting my wedding venue?"

Richard twitched one shoulder up and down. "That depends. Do you consider your mother flying here early to be better or worse than a hurricane?"

I dropped my purse on the floor, taking in the planning chaos and trying to imagine adding my mother into the mix.

Kate patted my arm. "It might not be too late to go get married in the middle of the hurricane."

CHAPTER 8

I stood in the kitchen with a box of brownie mix and a bowl on the counter in front of me.

"Really, darling?" Richard stood on the other side of the counter separating my kitchen and living room, a disapproving look on his face.

"You know baking calms me." I picked up the box and read the list of ingredients, hoping I had the scant few things it required.

He wrinkled his nose. "But from a box? I told you I could make you some from scratch."

I waved a hand at him. "Nope. You've done enough."

"You're upset I didn't talk your mother out of coming, aren't you?"

I didn't look up at him. Everyone else had cleared out after I'd had a mini meltdown and told them I needed the rest of the day off. "How did my mother know we'd changed the venue so quickly?"

He pressed a hand to his heart. "You wanted me to keep it from your mother? It's not like she can't see the weather report, Annabelle. The hurricane isn't a secret."

I ripped open the box and dumped the contents into the

bowl, sending up a plume of chocolate scented dust. "The last thing I need on top of everything is my mother trying to change my wedding."

Richard coughed as the brownie mix cloud reached him. "Why would she change it?"

I shot him a look. He knew very well that a stateside wedding meant that things could go from casual beachside to formal debutante in a heartbeat. "Don't play coy with me." I pointed a wooden spoon at him. "You told her she could come early, you get to keep her occupied for the rest of the week."

His mouth dropped open, then he straightened his shoulders. "That's fine. You know I adore your mother."

"Whose mother?" Reese's voice came from the door, and I craned my neck to see him walking in.

"Annabelle's mother is flying in to help," Richard said in a stage whisper, "And your fiancée isn't happy about it."

"I never said that," I called out. "I just said I didn't have time to keep her entertained with everything else on my plate."

There was a low rumble of voices in the living room as Richard and Reese talked quietly enough that I couldn't hear them. That was fine by me. I didn't want to hear any more of Richard's explanations. I turned and opened a cabinet door, locating the vegetable oil and feeling vindicated that I had enough. I found my measuring cup and carefully poured two thirds of a cup of the golden liquid into it and then into the bowl.

The front door opened and closed again as I swirled the oil into the powder, watching it became a velvety brown batter. When I looked up, my hot cop fiancé stood in the kitchen doorway watching me stir.

"Is it helping?" he asked.

I glanced back down at the batter. "A little, but I might need ten more boxes to make me forget that I have to deal with my mother all week."

Reese came up behind me and wrapped his arms around my waist, lowering his mouth to my ear. "You don't need to worry about your mother. I'm going to get her settled in her hotel when she arrives tomorrow and then Richard is going to take her out to lunch."

I let myself sink back into him, feeling the hardness of his muscles and slowing my stirring. "You don't have to do that."

"Don't be silly," he murmured, his lips buzzing against my earlobe. "Gwen loves me."

He was right about that. My mother adored my fiancé even more than she loved Richard, which was saying something. Of course, most women found Mike Reese's charms hard to resist. He was tall and darkly handsome with just enough of a mischievous smile to make him impossible to resist. "I know she loves you, but don't you have to work?"

He gave a small shrug. "I can go in early or work a little late. If it helps take some of the stress off you, I'm happy to do it, babe."

"You really don't have to."

"Remember, she's not my mom so she doesn't drive me crazy."

I sighed. "She doesn't drive me... okay, yes, she drives me crazy. But only because she has an opinion about everything in my life and her opinion is usually that I'm doing it wrong. You're just about the only thing I've done she's been impressed by."

"That's not true. I know she's proud that you've built such a successful business."

"She'd rather have grandkids than a career woman for a daughter."

Reese's hand slid over my stomach and his voice was a dark purr. "Who says she can't have both?"

I swatted at his hand. "Not yet! We aren't even married."

He pretended to look at a watch on his wrist that wasn't

there. "A technicality, babe. We'll be married in less than a week."

"If I survive this week." I let my head drop back and rest on his chest. "Between having to replan a wedding, coming to terms with our ceremony being officiated by Tequila Mockingbird, and dealing with a bride who's convinced her husband is missing, I don't think I can handle one more thing."

"Normally, I'd be more concerned about a drag queen marrying us, but what's this about a missing husband?"

I bit my lower lip. Shoot. I hadn't meant for that to slip. "It's probably nothing. One of our former brides is convinced something bad has happened to her husband, but Kate thinks the guy is probably shacked up with a floozy."

"Kate usually has pretty good instincts about men. Has the bride reported him missing?"

"She doesn't want to because of the publicity. Her husband is Brock McCoy."

Reese stiffened slightly. "The young guy with the political talk show?"

I nodded. "He went on a run and didn't come back, but the bride admitted that they'd been fighting. Kate thinks he left her."

"Chances are higher that he left, but she should report it." He squeezed my hand. "And *you* should not be involved at all."

"I know, but it's so hard to tell a bride no. Even if she's a past bride."

He let out a breath. "If you want, I can make a few very discreet inquiries. This does not mean that I'm sanctioning your involvement, but if it helps find the guy and get the whole mess off your to-do list, then I'll do it."

I blinked hard as tears stung the backs of my eyes. I knew he was offering to do this against his better judgment and only because he knew me too well. I took a shuddering breath. "What did I do to deserve you?"

He nipped at the top of my ear. "I think it's the other way around, babe."

I laughed. "I'm pretty sure, with my friends as part of the package, I definitely got the better deal."

Reese tightened his arms around my waist. "Are you kidding? Without Fern, how would I have learned how to properly manscape?"

I shook my head slowly. "Do I want to know?"

His laugh vibrated his lips against my neck. "Probably not."

Looking down, I realized that I was no longer stirring the batter as if I was punishing it for serious misdeeds. I dropped the spoon and turned to face him. "How do you do that?"

He traced a finger down the side of my face, his hazel eyes meeting mine. "Do what?"

"Make everything better."

He tipped my chin up and kissed me softly. "It's my job. Besides, you're always fixing things for everyone else. It's only fair that someone make things better for you."

Fresh tears pricked at the backs of my eyelids. "You know what?"

He kissed me again, this one lingering and sending frissons of electricity through me. "What?"

"I'm glad you asked me to marry you, Detective."

He smiled slowly, his eyes deepening to green as he pulled me closer. "That makes two of us."

My pulse fluttered and my breath quickened. "What would you say to running off and eloping?"

He pulled my hair out of its ponytail and tangled one hand in it. "I'd say we'd better run far enough that Richard couldn't find us. Ever."

As excited as Richard was to be both my Man of Honor and a groomsman, he might just hunt us to the ends of the Earth if we got married without him. "I guess we're going to have to go through with the wedding then."

"No matter what happens, babe, it will be the best wedding ever if I'm marrying you."

I jumped up into his arms and he caught me with one hand, as I wrapped my legs around his waist. "Tell me more."

His eyes flashed molten as he pulled my lips to his, kissing me as he walked out of the kitchen and down the hall.

CHAPTER 9

The next morning, I was dressed and mostly awake when Richard sailed into my apartment, leather crossbody bag slung over one shoulder with Hermès poking out one side.

He gave me a cursory glance and smirked. "Someone is in a better mood."

My cheeks warmed. "It's a wonder what a good night's sleep will do for you."

He deposited Hermès on the floor, and the Yorkie proceeded to scamper around and sniff the furniture as if it had changed since the day before. Sauntering into the kitchen, Richard eyed the bowl of uncooked brownie batter in the kitchen sink. "Mm hmm. I'll bet."

I ignored his smug expression and walked past him into the living room. I sank into my yellow twill couch and tucked my bare feet up under me. He was right. I was definitely feeling calmer since my mini meltdown the night before, and it had little to do with sleeping. My mind wandered to my fiancé and how deftly he'd taken my mind off wedding stress and reminded me why we were having a wedding in the first place. "I've regained my perspective, that's all. The wedding will be wonderful, no matter what."

Richard followed me, putting his man bag on the couch and smoothing the front of his crisp, green cotton shirt. "I'm glad, darling." He pulled some papers out of his bag. "Because we have some serious decisions to make—before your mother arrives."

That had me sitting up. "I almost forgot she was coming."

One of Richard's eyebrows twitched. "I'm not sure if you got perspective or amnesia."

"Thank you for keeping her busy, by the way. Reese told me that you two are tag teaming her today."

He grimaced for a moment. "That's not the phrase I would have used, but we are keeping Gwen occupied."

"She'll be thrilled. She loves both of you."

Richard smiled. "Of course, she does."

I took a long gulp of my bottled coffee, resisting the urge to roll my eyes. "So, what decisions do we need to make? I didn't get to hear much about your planning progress yesterday."

"Yes, well." He narrowed his eyes at me. "Aside from getting no help from Leatrice and Fern yesterday, I was able to locate some venue options."

"Good ones?" Washington might have lots of great places to hold a party, but they usually booked up months—sometimes well over a year—in advance.

He shoved a pile of wedding magazines to one side and fanned several contracts across the coffee table. "See for yourself."

I leaned forward. Somehow Richard had managed to get contracts from three different venues for Saturday. I pushed the one hotel contract aside. "I'd like to avoid a hotel if we can."

"You know I won't argue with you there. A hotel won't let Richard Gerard Catering provide the food, and you know how I feel about on-site cuisine."

I was very aware of Richard's opinions on just about everything, including hotel food, which—aside from some notable exceptions—he deemed ghastly. My eyes lingered on one of the two remaining contracts. "I think the Carnegie Institute would be perfect."

Even though the name—the Carnegie Institute for Science —wasn't exactly romantic, the building on 16th Street boasted a long flight of wide, marble stairs leading up to tall columns. Inside, there was a striking inlaid marble rotunda perfect for ceremonies and a long wood-paneled room that was ideal for an intimate dinner reception.

Richard handed me a pen. "You won't get any arguments from me. The girls who run the place are a delight."

I scanned the boilerplate contract language, making sure there were no hidden clauses that could come back to bite me later. I made a mental note of load-in times and the number of hours provided with the rental fee. Once I was satisfied, I signed my name on the last page with a flourish.

Richard snatched it from the table and tucked it into his bag. "I'll drop this off in person before I go see your mother."

I flopped back on the overstuffed couch cushions. "The Carnegie is a far cry from Jamaica, but at least my mother will be pleased. The venue is right up her alley."

Richard hesitated, meeting my gaze. "I know this isn't going to be much like you'd envisioned. I also know you aren't one of those brides who can't let go of their idealized wedding day, but are you going to be terribly unhappy not to be getting married with your feet in the sand?"

Hermès leapt onto the couch next to me—his inspection of the entire apartment apparently complete—and nuzzled my hand.

I ruffled the brown-and-black fur on his head. "Honestly, as long as I'm marrying Reese and my best friends are there, it doesn't matter where it happens."

Richard cleared his throat and fiddled with the straps on his man bag. "Good."

"Unless you're offering to ship in a truckload of sand and spread it over the rotunda at the Carnegie?"

Richard's head snapped up, and he inhaled sharply. "I'm doing no such thing."

I grinned at him from behind my bottled drink. "It was worth a try."

Richard mumbled something about bridezillas under his breath as my phone vibrated from where it sat on the edge of the coffee table, the screen facing up with an incoming text.

I reached for it, but Richard beat me to it, plucking it from the table and glancing down at the message.

"Nosy much?" I asked, watching his face assume a confused expression.

He held up my phone. "I know this Amanda."

I stifled a groan. Of course, he knew Amanda. He'd been involved in her wedding weekend, as well.

"Why is Amanda texting you a list of names?" He asked. "Why is she texting you at all? Her wedding was ages ago."

I tried to think of a convincing excuse but came up short, making a lunge for the phone instead. "It's nothing."

Richard gave me a stern look. "Annabelle, what have I told you about setting boundaries with clients?" His gaze dropped back to the phone screen. "Potential suspects? What is this? What's going on?" He sucked in a breath, dropping the phone onto the couch. "Please tell me you aren't..."

I guessed it was too horrible for Richard to utter out loud, but his wide eyes did not leave my face.

I scooped up my phone. "It's really nothing. Probably Amanda being neurotic."

"That I could believe, but what is she being neurotic about and what does it have to do with you?"

I scanned the text quickly, my stomach tightening as I read her brief message followed by a list of names. "Brock is kind of missing, so Kate and I went over to lend our moral support."

"Kind of missing?" Richard put one hand on his hip and

tapped a toe rapidly on the floor. "Isn't missing an absolute? Either you are or you aren't?"

"Not really. She might think he's missing, and he might be perfectly fine."

He crossed his arms over his chest. "But she thinks he's *not* fine, and you and Kate were doing more than just being supportive."

Now I folded my arms over my chest. "She doesn't want to get the police involved because of all the bad PR. Kate thinks it's because she's afraid he's actually shacked up with a floozy and Amanda doesn't want that to leak to the media."

"For once, I hope Kate is right." Richard nodded to my phone. "So why is she sending you a list of names?"

I dropped my gaze. "I might have said I'd make discreet inquiries if he didn't turn up."

"You told a former client you'd investigate her husband's disappearance the week of your own wedding?" His voice was dangerously calm.

"It's not a real investigation, and I promise it won't interfere with my wedding. Besides, Reese said he'd look into it for me —off the books. He took the route the groom always ran and is having some patrolmen check it out. So, you can forget running off and tattling to him about it."

Richard's mouth dropped open. "First of all, I am a grown man. I do not tattle." He plucked his bag off the couch along with Hermès and spun around to the door, glancing back over his shoulder and fixing me with a sharp look. "But I can still tell your mother."

CHAPTER 10

"*S*ee?" Kate glanced over at me as she drove down Georgetown Parkway, the car swerving slightly as she took her eyes off the road that cut through forest and skirted along above the Potomac River. "Another reason this is a horrible idea."

I braced my arms on the dash of her car, regretting my decision to preserve my excellent parking spot and let Kate drive. We were on the way to pick up my gown and her bridesmaid dress at Love Couture salon, which was located in an upscale suburb of the city. "He's not going to tell my mother. He was bluffing. He doesn't want my mother hysterical any more than I do."

Kate shot me another look that told me she wasn't so sure. "And it's okay that you're not meeting your mother when she arrives?"

"She'll be more excited to see Reese, anyway." I waved a hand at my ponytail, barely-there makeup, and casual, floral print dress. "This look would give her way too much to worry about."

Kate turned her attention back to the road. "Explain to me again how you managed to be so different from your mother."

I shrugged. I tried not to think too much about how far

from the tree I'd fallen. Moving to DC had made it easy to ignore the obvious differences with my debutante mother and feel less guilty about being a debutante dropout. The distance had also been a welcome respite from the sense that I was always coming up short, at least in the areas that seemed to matter to her. "Who knows? Recessive genes?"

Kate veered into the next lane without signaling, and a car behind us honked. "It must have killed her that you're so naturally pretty without even trying."

"I don't think it's that," I said, my face warming from the compliment. I was glad the air in the car was turned on high.

Kate shook her head. "Fern always says that's your charm. That you don't even know you're pretty and you never even try."

"Thanks, I think."

"But he also said that if you don't let him do something with your hair other than a bun or ponytail on your wedding day, he'll kill you."

I laughed. "I promise I won't walk down the aisle with a ponytail."

She let out a breath, leaning one elbow on the driver's side door. "That's a relief. Now, bring me up to speed on what Richard's done. He was a bit secretive yesterday."

"I think that's because he was spilling the beans to my mother and didn't want me to know. Other than that, he found a few venue options, and I signed the contract with Carnegie this morning."

Kate nodded slowly as she absorbed this information. "It's not a beach in Jamaica, but it's the perfect size. And that rotunda does make for beautiful photos."

"Now I just have to figure out if Fern was serious about officiating the ceremony in drag."

Kate's head swung around, and more cars honked as we swerved out of our lane. "How does he plan to get you ready and then run the ceremony?" She gave a brusque shake of her head. "I'll call someone from our list of officiants. There has to be someone available who'll be more sober than Fern will."

I remembered the ceremony he'd led dressed in full priest regalia and the rather rambling homily about shopping he'd given, thanks to a few too many glasses of champagne. "I think that's a good idea."

"Obviously Buster and Mack are still doing the decor, but it's going to be different now that it's not on an island."

I clutched the grip over the door as Kate exited the parkway faster than she should have "Tropicals don't exactly go with the sophisticated elegance of Carnegie, do they?"

She gave me a sad look. "This is completely changing your wedding, isn't it?"

"It's fine. Yes, I envisioned being barefoot on the beach, but I can't really control a hurricane, can I? And if I want to keep the wedding on the same date—which I do because otherwise we don't have a wedding-free weekend until winter—then I need to be flexible."

"And Reese is fine with all this?"

My throat was thick as I thought about my fiancé. "He says as long as he's marrying me, it doesn't matter where it is."

Kate let out a deep sigh. "You know I'm not the marrying type, but you really did get yourself a good one."

"I know. He wasn't even upset when I told him about Amanda."

Her jaw dropped. "You told him?"

I nodded, relaxing my death grip on the handle over my head. "He was actually pretty great about it. He said he'd poke into it without opening an official case."

"If Brock is still missing. My money's on the guy waltzing back in."

"Then you'd be out some cash." I took my phone out of my purse and tapped the screen. "As of this morning, he was still missing, and Amanda sent me a list of people she thinks could have a reason to want him gone."

Kate tightened her grip on the steering wheel as we merged onto the Beltway. "A list? I thought we agreed that this whole thing was a bad idea."

"My wedding has had to be completely changed because of a hurricane and my mother is in town," I said. "Trust me, I'd rather be thinking about a missing groom than the million ways this week has turned into a disaster."

She sighed. "Okay, but I'm only doing this because for some weird reason, solving crimes calms you."

"Distracts me," I corrected.

"Same thing," she said. "So how long is this list?"

I flashed the screen with at least a dozen names at her. "Mostly his TV competition."

"Other political pundits?" Kate cranked up the AC even higher. "Read them out and let's see if I know any."

Considering how widely Kate dated in the DC metropolitan area, this wasn't a bad plan. I knew she'd dated more than her fair share of both political types and TV stars. I started reading the names from top to bottom.

"Did you say Chaz Hunter?" Kate asked when I was only three names in. "The guy on that Sunday morning show about politics?"

I didn't tell her that "Sunday morning show about politics" wasn't very specific. "You know him?"

"A bit." She made a face. "We can eliminate him as a suspect."

"Any reason why?"

Kate shifted in her seat. "We went out a few times. He's way too mild-mannered to commit any sort of crime."

"That seems vague. We can't be eliminating suspects just because they were too boring for you."

She twitched one shoulder up. "Have it your way, but I'm telling you, he doesn't have it in him."

I usually trusted Kate's take on men since she had so much more experience with them. She could tell at a glance if a guy was cheating on his wife or girlfriend, and I'd never known her instincts to be wrong. I also knew that her gut feeling would be hard to justify to anyone who wasn't aware of her superpower. Still, I moved Chaz to the bottom of the list.

"It sounds like a bunch of these are from Brock's own network," Kate said after I read off two more names.

I scanned the list. "I guess. That would make the most sense, too."

Kate reached forward and activated the Bluetooth on her console, redialing a recently called number.

"Who are you calling?" I asked as the sound of ringing filled the car.

Before she could answer, a woman's voice came on. "Hey, Kate!"

I recognized the voice of one of our usual makeup artists, Nikki. "And Annabelle."

"Hey, ladies," Nikki said. "It sounds like you're in a car."

"You know us," Kate said in a louder voice than usual as she exited the beltway. "Always on the go."

"I hear that."

"So, do you still do the makeup down at channel 7?" Kate asked, barely glancing behind her as she took another exit and merged into fast traffic.

You're brilliant, I mouthed to my assistant. She was a horrific driver, but she was an amazing networker. Since Nikki was the regular makeup artist for the local TV station, she knew Brock McCoy—and who might have it in for him—better than almost anyone.

Thanks, Kate mouthed back, winking at me.

"You know it, girl," Nikki said. "But I still keep my weekends open for weddings."

"What's the scoop on Brock McCoy?" Kate asked.

"Brock?" Nikki's voice changed slightly. Was it my imagination or did she suddenly sound cautious? "Weren't you his planners?"

"We were," I chimed in. "And you did such an amazing job with all the makeup. And that was *not* an easy bridal party."

She laughed. "You got that right."

"We just wondered how he got along with everyone at the station," Kate said. "He was always great to us, but we only saw him for one day. I'll bet you see a lot more since you're at the station almost every day."

"Brock has always been nice to me," Nikki said, but that hesitation had crept back into her voice. "He treats the staff really well, and not everyone does. His publicist is intense, but she's new so everyone cuts her some slack."

The publicist must be new, because I didn't remember one at their wedding.

"So, he's not a diva?" I asked.

"He has a publicist," Kate muttered quietly. "What does that tell you?"

"He could be difficult," Nikki said. "But he's not. At least not to me. I know not all the other talent likes him, but that's just because he's younger and better looking than most of them."

She was right about that. Brock McCoy looked more like an anchor for an entertainment show than a political pundit. "I'll bet that pisses the old guys off."

She laughed. "Some of them, but it's politics. They're always yelling at each other over something."

"He gets in fights with other on air pundits?" Kate asked, swinging the car into an upscale shopping area.

"Sometimes," Nikki admitted. "Usually they keep it to the show, but last week they kept going after the cameras stopped rolling."

"Really?" I tried not to sound too eager. "Who was the guy he got into it with?"

"It wasn't a guy. It was a woman." Nikki took a noticeable breath before continuing. "Audra Duncan."

Kate flinched slightly as she pulled into a spot in front of

Love Couture Bridal Salon, the shop's large glass windows displaying mannequins in elaborate wedding gowns.

The name sounded familiar, but I wasn't sure why. "Who—?"

"Former White House Assistant Communications Director," Kate said, cutting off my question.

Suddenly, I remembered Audra Duncan. She was known for her striking beauty— and for being absolutely ruthless.

CHAPTER 11

"*T*his changes everything," Kate whispered, as we stepped inside the upscale bridal salon.

Even though we'd only had to walk a few steps from her car to the shop door, the July heat already had sweat beading on my upper lip, so I was grateful for the blast of arctic air that hit us when we pushed through the glass double doors.

"Why?" I studied her pinched expression. "Do you know Audra personally or something?"

"I'll tell you later," she whispered, as the doors closed behind us and we entered the quiet space that instantly felt more serene than the parking lot.

I inhaled the perfumed air, walking toward the white half-moon receptionist desk perched underneath a large sign that read "Love" in curving white letters on a field of dove-gray. Our shoes tapped on the glossy, dark wood floors, announcing our arrival even if the tinkling bell over the door hadn't.

"There's the bride." A tall, thin woman with sleek brown hair came out from behind the desk with her arms open wide.

For a moment, I glanced around looking for the bride until I realized that she meant me. No matter how long I was engaged, I still couldn't get used to the idea of being the bride.

"Hi Caroline," I said, giving the salon owner a hug. "I guess that's me, right?"

"Of course, it's you." She shook her head as she hugged Kate, then dropped her voice to a conspiratorial whisper. "Wedding planners make the worst brides, don't they?"

I opened my mouth to protest, but Caroline was already waving us back toward the fitting rooms.

"Your dress is altered and pressed and in a bag." Caroline led us down a hallway that had one wall of glass and another of shiny black dressing room doors. At the end, a white garment bag with the shop logo hung on the outside of one of the doors. "It should travel well, but be sure to take it out of the bag and hang it up as soon as you reach the island."

"There's not going to be any island or any traveling," I said.

Caroline stopped and spun around, putting a hand to her mouth. "What? Don't tell me you and the hot cop—?"

"No, nothing like that." I shook my head quickly at her stricken expression. "We're still getting married."

Caroline sank onto a nearby ivory tufted bench. "Thank goodness. I thought I'd stuck my foot in it again. I've only had a handful of weddings called off last-minute and one called it off then back on again."

"The wedding is definitely on," Kate said. "But there's a hurricane moving over Jamaica, so we had to move it to DC."

Caroline's face brightened. "As long as you're still walking down the aisle, that's good news." She cut her eyes to the garment bag. "And your gown is classic enough that it will look beautiful even if you aren't on the beach."

I smiled, remembering the simple, ivory organza dress I'd chosen with an A-line skirt and spaghetti straps. Even though it would have been perfect for a wedding in the sand, it would also translate well to a ceremony in the rotunda of the Carnegie.

"One thing you do need now," Caroline said, dropping her gaze to my feet.

"Shoes," Kate and I said in unison.

Caroline grinned. "You were supposed to be barefoot on the beach. I'm guessing your new DC venue is not a shoes optional type of place."

"Not exactly," I said. "It would be a little odd if the bride was the only person not wearing shoes."

"And your mother would keel over," Kate added under her breath.

"So now you need wedding shoes." Caroline stood, plucking the long garment bag off the door and heading back toward the front of the salon, flipping her long hair behind her. "We keep the shoes at the front."

Kate and I trailed behind her, walking to an open space with a small, round stage surrounded on three sides by tall mirrors. Glass shelving units lined the walls, each level displaying bridal shoes or jewelry.

"Since you'd planned to be barefoot, you shouldn't wear a high heel," Caroline said, inspecting the displays. "Otherwise, the gown won't be long enough."

"And no one wants a high-water wedding dress," Kate said.

The salon owner held up a kitten heel sandal with straps crisscrossing the front. "What about this?"

I took it from her. "I like it. It's simple and not too fussy."

Caroline fluttered a hand dismissively toward the more ornate shoes with glittering jewels encrusting the toes. "Those aren't you at all. What size are you?"

"Eight," I told her, as she took the sample back and replaced it on the clear stand.

She swung her gaze to Kate. "What about you? You were going to be barefoot, too, weren't you?"

Kate muttered a curse under her breath. "That's right. I'd almost forgotten we were picking up my dress, as well."

"Don't worry. I wouldn't have let you walk out without your dress." Caroline eyed us both. "This hurricane really has you two flustered."

"I wish it was only a hurricane we were dealing with," Kate muttered.

I shot my assistant a look, but it was too late. Caroline dealt with brides on a regular basis, so she was skilled at picking up emotional undercurrents.

"Don't tell me you two are caught up in some sort of drama again?" Her eyes sparkled with interest. Caroline had been a source of clues during a murder investigation not too long ago. Since she got to know our brides and oftentimes their families and bridal party as they tried on dresses, she could be a fount of information. In lay terms, she overheard a lot of dirt.

"Nothing like a murder," I said, quickly.

Kate bobbled her head. "We actually don't know what it is yet. Right now, it's just a missing groom."

Caroline inhaled sharply. "For one of your upcoming weddings? How horrible."

"Actually, it's a former groom," I said. "They got married about six months ago."

Caroline tilted her head at us. "And you're involved…?"

"An excellent question," Kate said. "The simplest answer is that Annabelle can't say no to a client, even if they aren't a client anymore."

Caroline gave me a sympathetic look. "It's hard to tell them no. I get that." Her gaze shifted to the shoes again, and she ran her hands over a selection of metallic sandals. "Is this one of my brides, as well?"

I thought back quickly and shook my head. "It's one of the few we didn't bring to you. The bride was a beauty queen and used her pageant gown designer for her wedding dress, so you wouldn't know her."

Caroline tapped her chin, picking up a strappy silver sandal with a low heel. "What about this for Kate?"

Kate flicked her gaze to it then away. "Add about three inches of heel, and we're in business."

Caroline replaced the shoe and picked up another with a spike heel. "Do you mean Amanda Hart?"

Kate and I both gaped at her, then Kate glanced down at the shoe. "That's perfect. I'm a seven and a half. And how did you know that?"

Caroline waved a hand at us, smiling. "I did her sister's wedding, so I remember her from the fittings."

Kate nodded slowly. "That's right. Her sister got married a year or two before Amanda, but we didn't do the wedding."

"No shock there. It wasn't nearly the extravagant affair Amanda's was," Caroline said. "If I remember correctly, the bride's family wasn't thrilled about the guy she was marrying."

I tried to recall the sister of the bride's husband, but I drew a blank. We saw so many people on a wedding day—especially a large wedding like Amanda's with a big bridal party and hundreds of guests—that it was hard to remember individuals unless they did something very memorable. And since the Hart-McCoy wedding had been black tie, the sister's husband had been one of the two hundred plus men in penguin suits.

"Why?" Kate sat down on a backless sofa with rolled ends and stretched her legs in front of her.

Caroline disappeared into a door leading to the back of the shop and, I suspected, their supply of shoes in different sizes. She yelled something, but it was hard to hear her.

"What did she say?" I asked Kate, as I joined her on the couch.

My assistant shrugged. "You know, I think I remember the guy now that Caroline mentioned it. He's good looking, but shifty."

"Shifty? In what way?

"I don't remember more than a feeling, but I remember that he wasn't one of the groomsmen, and he was kind of lingering in the back of everything."

I tried to think back the day, but I didn't remember a shifty guy. Then again, Kate was always more attuned to the men at weddings than I was.

Caroline reappeared from the back holding two shoe boxes. "I've got your sizes."

"What were you saying about the guy the sister married?" I asked, taking one of the shoe boxes from her.

"I don't know the details," she said, her cheeks flushing slightly, "but I do know that the guy had a record."

"A record?" I dropped the shoe I'd taken out of the box. "As in, the brother-in-law is a criminal?"

CHAPTER 12

"*H*ow did we not know this?" I asked, carefully stretching two garment bags across Kate's backseat.

Kate tucked the glossy shopping bag with our shoe boxes behind the passenger's seat. "Why would we? It's not like our clients give us a dossier on their entire families before we start working with them."

"Maybe we should start doing a little more research." I lowered myself into the car, keeping the door open until Kate could get in and crank up the AC. It was almost noon, and the overhead sun was punishing.

"There's always Leatrice."

I groaned. My elderly downstairs neighbor would love nothing more than to do questionably legal investigations of my clients, but I couldn't be sure that she wouldn't end up tailing them in ridiculous disguises. The last thing I needed was a bunch of brides who were paranoid they were being followed.

I hurriedly fastened my seatbelt as Kate jerked the car into gear. "It's too bad Caroline didn't know what kind of crime he was convicted for."

"I'm guessing something white collar. Ava wouldn't marry

someone convicted of murder, even if she does want to shock her family."

I cut my eyes to Kate. "You think she married a guy with a record on purpose?"

Kate twitched one shoulder up and down. "The sister always struck me as the type who was trying to catch up to her older sister but could never quite do it. Wasn't she just first runner up in her pageant, while Amanda was Miss Whatever?"

"Miss Ohio."

Kate fluttered a hand absently, as she merged onto the beltway amid a cacophony of honking. "Whatever. Maybe Ava decided to try to get attention in a different way."

I clutched the door handle. "Marrying a convict is an interesting way to do it."

"There are stranger ways, trust me."

I knew Kate enough that I didn't want to ask. "Even if the brother-in-law has a criminal background, that doesn't mean he had anything to do with the groom going missing."

"Agreed." Kate adjusted her air conditioning vents and leaned closer, so the air blew her hair away from her face. "I'm still not convinced the guy hasn't run off to Cancún to start a life with a less high maintenance woman."

I shot her a look, but I couldn't completely disagree with her. Over the course of planning her wedding, Amanda had been a lot to handle. She'd never been rude or irrational, but she was used to getting her way. In all the months we'd worked with the couple, I'd never seen the groom make a wedding-related decision. Not that he seemed to care. He'd been way more focused on his burgeoning career, which was why I couldn't completely buy Kate's theory. He might have given up on his marriage, but I seriously doubted the guy would abandon his career.

"What about the fight with Audra Duncan?" I asked. "Earlier, you seemed convinced that was significant."

Kate cringed. "Wishful thinking on my part."

I released my grip on the door handle. "Okay, you have to spill it. What's your deal with Audra? Do you know her?"

Kate let out a slow breath and shifted in her seat. "When I first moved to DC, it was because of my ex-boyfriend."

I twisted so I could fully face her. "Wait, what? I never knew this. You had a boyfriend serious enough to move for?"

She didn't meet my gaze. "It was years ago, and I was a lot younger and much dumber, but yes. I moved my entire life for a guy."

I studied Kate's clenched jaw and the knuckles white on her steering wheel. It was hard to imagine Kate, who made it a point to never get too attached to any one guy, rearranging her life for a boyfriend. As a matter of fact, I didn't think Kate had had an official boyfriend since I'd known her. Sure, she dated non-stop, but she never stuck with anyone long enough for them to be called a boyfriend. I suspected I was about to find out why. "So, what happened?"

She laughed, but it was forced. "The same thing that always happens. It didn't work out, and I was left in a city where I knew no one with no place to live and no job."

I thought back to how I'd hired her to be my assistant. "But you knew Fern."

She grinned. "Actually, I didn't. Not really, but I walked into his salon after everything imploded determined to change my life by changing my hair. I used to have long hair, you know."

I didn't know, but I tried not to let my mouth hang open any more than it already was.

"Anyway," Kate went on, "Fern started cutting, and I started telling him my sob story. By the end, he'd given me a bob and told me that he knew of a wedding planner who needed an assistant. The rest is history."

"How have I never known this?" I shook my head in disbelief. "I thought Fern knew you from the wedding industry. At least, that's what he made it sound like."

"I think he felt sorry for me and knew I just needed someone to take a chance on me."

I twisted back around to face forward, trying to absorb everything. I reached out and put my hand over one of hers. "Well, I'm glad he lied."

"I think he would call it embellishing the truth. But I'm glad, too." She squeezed my hand back. "And I'm glad you didn't check references and took a chance on me."

I pulled back my hand and cleared my throat. "So now that we've established I hired an assistant who had zero wedding experience, what does this have to do with Audra Duncan? I'm assuming there's a connection?"

Kate snapped her fingers. "Right. Sorry. My ex-boyfriend and I broke up because he was cheating on me with this bleached blond tramp who was clawing her way up the political ladder."

"Audra Duncan."

Kate nodded, but didn't look over at me.

"And you've had to watch this woman in the news for years," I said. "That must be awful."

"It's why I never watch the news. One of the reasons, at least."

I hesitated to ask my next question. "And did they stay together? Audra and your ex?"

Kate shook her head and her hair swung from side to side. "She dumped him not long after she blew up our relationship. I think she did it just out of spite. Before she came along, we'd been dating for two years and were planning to get engaged."

"What happened to your ex? Is he still around?"

Kate tightened her grip on the wheel. "She actually black-balled him after they broke up. Last I heard, he was working for some state legislature campaign in Utah."

I grimaced. "She does not sound like someone you want to cross." My phone trilled in my purse before Kate could respond. I pulled it out and answered it when I saw my fiancé's number flash on the screen.

"Babe," he said, his voice low and hushed.

"Let me guess," I said, a grin making my mouth tremble. "You're still with my mother."

"Actually, I just left her. Passed her off, I should say. Richard has taken her to lunch and then he's taking her to get her hair done with Fern."

I let out a relieved sigh. "That should eat up most of the day." I paused. "If Richard is with her, why do you still sound so stressed?"

"Do you remember how you gave me that political TV guy's usual jogging route?"

"Yes." I felt my stomach clench. "Why?"

"Well, I sent out some uniformed officers like I promised. I didn't give them details but I told them there was a missing runner."

I felt Kate's eyes on me. "And?"

"They found something, babe."

My throat went dry. "A body?"

"No body," he said, "but we did find the guy's phone off to the side of the path."

"What does that mean?" My voice cracked.

My fiancé let out a deep sigh. "It means that the guy probably isn't shacked up with a girlfriend. And this is now an official police investigation."

CHAPTER 13

"I'm so glad I saw you when you were coming in."
Leatrice sat across from me in my living room with Richard's dog, Hermès, on her lap. She wore a Hawaiian print shirt over beige pedal-pushers with what looked like a shell necklace dangling from her neck.

"Yes," Kate said, walking out from the kitchen and handing me a bottled Frappuccino. "Lucky us."

I gave her a look, hoping Leatrice didn't pick up on her sarcastic tone. "You look festive." I glanced at the little Yorkie, who wore a tiny lei around his neck. "I'm guessing Richard didn't drop him off wearing that."

Leatrice giggled and patted the dog on the head. "No. I was saving the lei for him to wear in Jamaica, but there's no need to do that anymore."

I hadn't known that Hermès had been planning to attend my Caribbean wedding, but there wasn't much point in bringing that up now. I took the cold bottle from Kate, grateful for the drink even though I wasn't sure I needed to be any more wired than I already was.

Leatrice pointed one wrinkled hand at the shopping bag I'd dropped by the couch before flopping down onto it. "Looks like you girls did some wedding shopping."

"Just picking up the dresses and shoes." Kate took the other end of the couch, flashing lots of bare leg when she crossed them.

Leatrice nibbled the corner of her thumbnail. "I hope my dress is still appropriate."

Since my downstairs neighbor was known for her eccentric outfits, there was a good chance it wouldn't have been appropriate even in Jamaica. Not that I would be bothered by her wardrobe choice. I'd learned to roll with the punches when it came to Leatrice. As long as she didn't surveil my guests in a trench coat and fedora, I'd be happy.

I glanced at the phone in my lap again. Reese had promised to call me after he spoke to Amanda, and I was nervous to hear how the bride had taken the news.

"You look a bit jittery, dear," Leatrice said. "I didn't take you for a nervous bride. You know you don't have a thing to fret over. My Sidney Allen is going to get you the best entertainment possible."

I took a long swallow of my drink. I tried not to think too hard about Leatrice's husband, who was more of a diva than any of his performers who strutted around in feathered headdresses. His style of entertainment wasn't exactly what I'd had in mind for my relaxed wedding, but I also didn't want to offend Leatrice.

"Has Sidney Allen run his plans by Richard?" Kate asked. "You know he's taken charge of the planning."

Leatrice patted a hand to her unnaturally dark hair. "I'm sure those two will work it out."

A more realistic scenario involved Richard and Sidney Allen rolling around on the ground trying to poke each other's eyes out. As I knew from experience, a wedding could only handle one diva at a time.

"It's not so much the wedding," I admitted, knowing that Leatrice would sniff out the case one way or another. I'd given up trying to hide our criminal investigations from her. She always found out anyway, and sometimes she provided excellent insight. "One of our former clients is missing and there's a possibility that foul play was involved."

Leatrice sat up, her eyes twinkling with unmasked delight. "Foul play?" She leaned forward, jostling Hermès so that he yipped. "Murder?"

I shook my head, refusing to say the word. "I didn't say that. There isn't a body, or any evidence of the groom being hurt."

Kate made a noise in her throat that told me she thought I was being naive, but I ignored her.

"The police found his cell phone — turned off."

Leatrice put her bony fingers to her lips. "Where did they find it?"

"On his usual running route through Rock Creek Park."

Leatrice's eyes widened. "That's a good place to kill someone and hide a body."

"There's no body," I insisted.

Leatrice gave me a sympathetic look that told me she thought I was fooling myself. "Of course, dear."

"At least we don't need to worry about it anymore," Kate said. "Now that Reese and the DC police department are on the case, we are officially off it." Her gaze locked on mine. "Right, Annabelle?"

"Sure," I said. "I just hope the police don't jump to conclusions."

"What conclusions would that be?" Leatrice asked.

I put my glass bottle on the coffee table. "You know how it goes. Husband goes missing. Wife is the chief suspect."

"It doesn't look great for her that she delayed reporting him missing," Kate muttered.

I narrowed my eyes at her. "Because she thought he might have run off after their fight and didn't want the scandal to hit the media. Even you said there was more of a chance he was shacked up with another woman than in danger."

Kate shrugged. "When I'm wrong, I'm wrong."

"Anyway," I said. "Why would she get us involved if she did something to the guy?"

Leatrice crinkled her bright coral lips. "That's a good point. You two are notorious for solving crimes. If she wanted to get away with a crime, she would be foolish to get the wedding planners of death involved."

I groaned at the nickname. "Please don't call us that."

"I think it makes you sound exciting and dangerous." Leatrice's eyes were wide.

"Not exactly two words most brides use when describing their ideal wedding planner," Kate said.

"So, what are the next steps?" Leatrice asked.

"For us?" Kate stood, plucking my empty bottle from the table and heading toward the kitchen. "Nothing. We let Annabelle's hunky fiancé do his job and we focus on our job— getting ready to marry off our girl."

"Technically, Richard is handling that," I said.

"And you want to give him free rein?" Kate asked from the kitchen, poking her head through the open space between the two rooms.

I hesitated. I trusted Richard implicitly, but I wasn't sure about giving him carte blanche when it came to my wedding.

"He has been talking to your mother," Kate reminded me.

"I can always help you with the case while you focus on the wedding," Leatrice said. "You know I have my online contacts."

"No," Kate and I said at the same time.

Leatrice's online contacts were hackers she'd met on the dark web. Even though they'd helped us before, I was reluctant to bring Boots and Dapper Dan into the mix, especially if it was an official police case. Reese did not look kindly upon Leatrice's connection to the seedy underbelly of the World Wide Web.

Leatrice opened her mouth to argue, but before she could,

Kate's phone rang, and my front door swung open. My jaw dropped as I saw Fern standing in the doorway—with my mother.

I jumped up from the couch, smoothing the front of my wrinkled cotton dress. "Mom, what are you—?"

"Surprise, honey!" She swept into my apartment on a cloud of Shalimar perfume, the rings on her fingers glittering as she pulled me into a hug.

"I finished her hair and we thought it would be fun to surprise you," Fern said, fluttering his hand toward my mother's shellacked, brown bob, which looked absolutely no different than it always did.

I was speechless as she held me at arm's length, looking me up and down and smiling. "I'm so glad you're having a comfortable day."

"Comfortable" was code for "dressed like a slob" in my mother's book. I heard Kate talking to someone in the kitchen, but I was too distracted by my mother to make out words.

My mother's gaze swept the room, landing on Leatrice, who'd jumped to her feet. "And this is your building superintendent, isn't it?"

Hermès had leapt to the floor and was dutifully sniffing my mother's Ferragamo pumps.

"Not exactly," I said, although Leatrice was much more on top of what went on in the building than the manager.

"Lovely to see you again," my mother said as she shook Leatrice's hand. "Thank you for keeping an eye on my Annabelle."

Leatrice looked slightly stunned, but did what most people did in my mother's presence—smiled and nodded.

I shot daggers at Fern, whose pupils widened. *What?* he mouthed, giving me his most innocent look.

"Just for this, I'm wearing a ponytail down the aisle," I hissed.

He pressed a hand to his throat. "You wouldn't."

I glared at him. "Try me."

Kate had emerged from the kitchen, and I noticed my mother flinch as she took in my assistant's short skirt. At least with Kate and Leatrice in the mix, my mother couldn't hone in on my clothing choices so much.

"Hi, Mrs. Archer," Kate said with a wave. "Good to see you again."

"How nice to see you, Katherine." My mother was too Southern to be anything less than perfectly polite, but I could tell that Kate's outfit was about to give her an eye twitch.

Luckily, Kate either didn't notice my mother's disapproval or didn't care, which made me love my assistant even more. She waved her cell phone in the air, and I grabbed for the lifeline.

"A client?" I asked, hopefully.

"Buster and Mack need to see us to go over final details before they place the floral order."

That would work, too. "I'll get my purse."

"The florists?" My mother asked, obviously remembering the names from when she'd met them at my engagement party. "Aren't they doing your wedding flowers?"

"Yes," I said slowly, before I could think of a convincing lie.

She hitched her own purse higher on her shoulder. "Then let's go. I have so many ideas now that you're not running off to an island like a hippie."

My mother swept out of my apartment, and I stepped closer to Fern, dropping my voice to a deadly whisper. "Run fast and run far."

CHAPTER 14

"I think this calls for a round of cappuccinos." Mack beamed at us as we perched on stools around the long metal table at the back of his floral shop.

Kate leaned her elbows on the shiny surface of the table. "I think I'm good, thanks."

Despite the air conditioning blasting in the shop, we'd just come in from the sweltering summer heat. I glanced over my shoulder at the wall lined with galvanized metal buckets of fresh flowers. At least the brightly hued roses, lilies, and hydrangea looked crisp, while I felt like the heat had sucked all the life out of me. "None for me, either."

"A cappuccino would be lovely," my mother said, setting her designer purse on the stool next to her.

Mack turned on his heel and bustled off to the coffee station behind him, the large chrome machine gleaming.

"Isn't this darling?" My mother craned her neck to take in the round display tables crowded with summer-themed topiaries, pastel scented candles, and nautical decor items. A rustic flower cart was positioned near the front entrance, bunches of yellow and white blooms spilling over the edges.

I breathed in the scent of flowers that now mingled with the rich aroma of coffee as Mack prepared a cappuccino for my mother. Luckily, the machine squealed loudly as he frothed the milk, preventing us from carrying on a conversation. This was a good thing, since we'd run out of small talk on the short drive across Georgetown.

"Here you are." Mack returned to the table, setting a large china cup in front of my mother. He put his own smaller espresso in front of him as he sat across from us, the chrome stool groaning from his weight. "Like I mentioned to Kate on the phone, Buster and I were able to cancel the flower order flying down to Jamaica since they couldn't actually get the plane there, but we do need to put in any final changes today."

"The only things we need to change are the ceremony flowers," I said before anyone else could speak. "There won't be a floral arch on the beach anymore."

He leaned his thick forearms on the rolled edge of the table as he flipped open my file. "We're at the Carnegie now, correct?"

I nodded. "Ceremony in the rotunda."

Mack stroked one hand down his goatee, a habit of his when he thought. "So, no arch?"

"A beauty arch doesn't fit without a beach," I said. "Just something simple and pretty."

"Annabelle," my mother said in a stage whisper. "I understand why you couldn't find a church on the island, but surely there must be a church available here. We passed a couple of charming ones on the way here."

"Christ Church?" Kate stifled a laugh, referencing one of the historic stone churches we'd driven by. "Good luck getting in there. If the scary church ladies didn't make you run away screaming first."

My mother looked confused, but I knew Kate was right. Not only did most churches book out at least six months in advance, they were much too strict for my liking. I'd spent enough time tiptoeing around church ladies for work. No way was I doing it on my own wedding day.

"It's too late to book a church," I said. "Besides, Reese and I want something less formal."

My mother made a disapproving noise in the back of her throat, and I wasn't sure if it was because of the church situation or me referring to my fiancé by his last name or both. "I'm sure Michael wouldn't oppose a church ceremony."

Mack's eyebrows popped up. I don't think any of us had ever heard Mike Reese referred to as Michael. He cleared his throat and regained his composure. "Annabelle is right, Mrs. Archer. It's too late to find a church, but Buster and I will make sure that your daughter's ceremony is spectacular."

"Thank you, Mackenzie. This wedding is a big deal to her father and me, you know." She gave me a pointed look. "And she's only doing this once."

I ignored Kate's shaking shoulders next to me. "You don't have to worry about that, mother."

Buster stepped out from the back of the shop, smiling broadly when he saw us and shifting the fair-haired toddler on his hip. "We thought we heard guests, didn't we, Merry?"

Merry gave us a shy smile, her eyes lighting on Mack as she clapped her hands.

Mack took the little girl from Buster, settling her on his broad lap. "Can you say hello, Merry?"

The little girl that Buster and Mack had become surrogate fathers to whispered hello to us, then buried her face in his leather jacket.

My mother put her hands to her cheeks. "Isn't she the most precious thing?" Her eyes went from Buster to Mack. "Whose is she?"

"Both of ours," Buster said. Since the two floral designers had found the baby on their doorstep and decided to give her —as well as her teenaged mother—a home, they considered themselves both her adopted fathers.

My mother's expression only faltered for a moment. "Well, she's adorable. And her name's Mary?"

"With an E and two Rs. As in Merry Christmas." Mack kissed the top of the girl's head. "She was a December baby."

Another sigh from my mother. At least this had distracted her from the fact that her only daughter wasn't getting married in a church, although I could sense what was coming next.

"I wouldn't mind becoming a grandmother before I die," she said, cutting her eyes to me.

I fought the urge to remind her that she would not have been pleased to become a grandmother before I was married.

"Do you mind if I hold her?" my mother asked.

"Of course not." Mack stood and walked around the table, while my mother slipped off her stool and held out her arms. He handed Merry over, and shockingly, the toddler didn't put up a fuss. She studied my mother, poking a chubby finger at her diamond stud earrings before apparently deciding that she would do.

My mother started to talk to Merry in a sing-song voice I'd never heard before, as she walked her around the shop, pointing at various objects and letting the little girl lean over to smell the different flowers in the metal buckets.

Mack jerked his head toward my file, lowering his voice to a whisper. "Let's finish this before she makes a full lap."

Kate and I twisted back around as Mack returned to his seat and chugged the rest of his espresso.

Buster sat next to him, squinting at the marked up proposal. "Carnegie, eh? Well, the tropicals won't work, will they?"

Kate glanced over her shoulder. "And Mom would rather the rotunda look like a cathedral."

Buster grinned at me. "Well, we can't have that, can we?"

I shook my head, keeping one eye on my mother's progress around the store's perimeter. "I may not be able to get married on the beach, but I don't want an old South wedding. Not that I don't love the South."

Mack reached over and patted my hand. "We know what you mean, sweetie."

Buster gave me a quick wink. "I know you love Sahara roses."

"And peonies," Kate added. "She's nuts about peonies."

Mack tapped his pen on his chin. "And you're actually at the best time for peonies. It's such a short window unless we fly them in."

Buster adjusted the motorcycle goggles on his bald head. "Do you trust us, Annabelle?"

"You know I do."

He closed the file and gave me a single nod. "Then don't worry about a thing. Mack and I will make everything perfect —and totally you."

My eyes stung as I blinked quickly. At this rate, I'd be an emotional wreck by the end of the week. "Thanks, guys."

The tinkling bell over the door made us all turn as Richard flounced into the store. He stopped short when he saw my mother holding Merry, giving the baby a pat on the head like he would give his dog.

"I see you're already hitting up your mother for babysitting," he said, when he'd joined us at the back.

"What are you doing here?" I asked.

"I'm supposed to be rescuing you." He eyed me. "Although you look fine to me."

"Rescuing me —?" I exchanged a look with Kate.

"Fern?" she asked.

Richard twitched one shoulder up without answering directly. "All I know is I'm here to take your mother out to dinner."

"That sounds fun," Mack said. "Can we join you?"

Richard's face froze, and I knew he was already calculating how a toddler would fit in at the presumably fancy restaurant he'd selected for dinner.

"How am I going to explain not having dinner with her?" I asked in a hushed voice.

Kate stole a glance at my mother. "I don't know if she'll care as long as Merry is there."

Richard pressed his lips together. This was clearly not going according to his plan.

"Tell her your fiancé is whisking you off somewhere," Kate said. "Michael seems to do no wrong in her book."

My phone vibrated in my pocket and I pulled it out, feeling a rush of pleasure when I saw that it was, in fact, Reese calling. "Speak of the devil."

"Hey, babe," he said when I answered.

Even though I thrilled at the familiar husk of his voice, I could tell something was wrong. "Hey, you. What's up?"

"I wanted you to hear it from me," he said. "We're bringing in your former bride as a suspect in the disappearance of her husband."

CHAPTER 15

I pushed open the door to my apartment and paused with my hand on the knob. Leatrice and her husband, Sidney Allen, were on my couch and Fern sat across from them, several cardboard pizza boxes open between them on the coffee table. Leatrice still wore a Hawaiian print shirt, but Sidney Allen was in a navy-blue suit, the jacket open across his expansive stomach.

"Annabelle!" Fern jumped up and hurried over to me, taking me by the arm and walking me inside. "I hope the cavalry arrived in time."

"You mean Richard?" I dropped my purse on the floor and let him lead me to an overstuffed chair.

Fern bobbed his head up and down, but not a hair slipped out of his low ponytail. "I thought he was the best choice for a rescue. Your paramour was too busy taking someone in for questioning."

He cut his eyes to the kitchen, and I spotted Reese's dark hair in the open space between the two rooms. I'd wondered if he would be done questioning Amanda by the time I extricated myself from the floral meeting and my mother.

Luckily, Merry had been enough of a distraction that my

mother had barely noticed when I'd told her I needed to get some work done.

"Your sweetie looked done in when he came home, so I offered to order pizza," Leatrice said, nodding at the kitchen timer on the table. "Unfortunately, they're getting faster with their delivery, so no free pies tonight."

"They're on to you, Honeybun," Sidney Allen said, patting her on the leg and looking at his wife adoringly.

I knew Leatrice was a stickler with her timer, and ate more than her fair share of free pizza. I also suspected the Georgetown pizza joints were getting wise to her. I eyed the open boxes, inhaling the delicious scent of melted cheese and Italian meats. "After my day, pizza sounds perfect."

Leatrice gave me a knowing look. "Don't worry, dear. I knew you wouldn't be cooking anyway."

Reese choked back a laugh as he walked out of the kitchen holding a glass of wine and a bottle of beer by the neck.

I narrowed my eyes at him, partly for laughing at Leatrice's dig about my cooking and partly for hauling my bride in for questioning.

He must have suspected that I'd be miffed with him because he handed me the wine and leaned in for a quick kiss. "Hey, babe. I thought you'd need this."

Even the brief contact with his lips made mine tingle, and the smell of his aftershave sent a small jolt down my spine. How did he do that to me every time? The man was so sexy it was maddening. I took a big gulp of white wine, hoping it would distract me from how appealing he was.

"Between my mother trying to convince me to change the wedding to a cathedral and you suspecting my bride of foul play, it's been a little stressful."

Reese leaned against the arm of my chair and rubbed my back, which did not help cool me off in the least.

"A cathedral?" Fern's eyes brightened.

Leatrice visibly perked up, as well. "Foul play?"

"I thought your wedding had been rebooked to the Carnegie Institute?" Sidney Allen slicked his thinning hair across his forehead.

"It has." Reese's hand on my back was comforting, and I allowed myself to lean into him. "I think we successfully convinced my mother that we can't find a church on such short notice, even if I wanted a church wedding."

"Good." Sidney Allen shimmied his pants up higher over his broad waist, confirming my theory that he would soon be buckling his belt around his neck. "I don't want to have to work around church ladies."

Before I could ask him why he'd need to worry about church ladies for my wedding, Fern handed me a slice of sausage and green pepper pizza. My hunger outweighed my curiosity, as I took a big bite of the gooey slice.

"Funny," my fiancé said, swigging his beer. "Gwen didn't mention anything about a church to me."

"Gwen?" I looked up at him, swallowing and shaking my head. "Of course, she didn't."

He grinned and arched an eyebrow, making me want to both punch him and kiss him. "You know, babe, as much as your mother drives you crazy, I think she's just happy for us and wants to be a part of everything."

"I'm happy for her to be a part of things," I said. "As long as she doesn't try to change everything. That's why we kept the wedding small and are paying for it ourselves." I pointed my pizza slice at him. "You are officially the first thing I've done that she's ever approved of."

He gave me a smug smile. "Maybe because she knows I'll take care of you and keep you out of trouble. I get the sense that you've been giving her the same fits you give me for years."

I elbowed him. "Just because I'm independent doesn't mean I need to be taken care of."

"Stubborn," he mumbled from behind his beer. "Not to mention a trouble magnet."

I gasped. "I heard that, and it is *so* not true."

He tilted his head at me. "Who got themselves involved in a criminal investigation days before their own wedding?"

I opened my mouth then closed it again. "It wasn't a criminal investigation when I got involved."

"That may be his point, sweetie," Fern said.

"Well, I was just trying to help out a client. My business runs on personal recommendations. I can't just ignore a bride, even if her wedding is over."

"You can if you aren't being paid," Sidney Allen said. "In the entertainment field, it's crucial to keep a line between business and friendship."

Leatrice gazed up at him and squeezed his chubby leg. "My Cupcake is such a smart businessman."

I knew that theory applied to events, too, but I'd always had a problem separating the two. Maybe because my best friends worked with me and all my weekends were spent at other people's parties.

I looked up at Reese. "You can't tell me you honestly suspect that Amanda had something to do with her husband's disappearance. She was hysterical when she called me to ask for my help. They've only been married for six months."

He shrugged. "I'm not saying she's involved, but the spouse is naturally a suspect, even one who seems upset."

"There are other people who make better suspects." I took a final drink of my wine. "Did you know that the bride's brother-in-law has a criminal record? Or that the groom got in a big fight with Audra Duncan down at the TV station?"

My fiancé twisted to face me fully. "How do you know all this? I thought you and Kate were picking up your wedding gown today."

My cheeks warmed. "We were, but that doesn't mean we can't talk to people. And the owner of the bridal salon happened to know that Amanda's family wasn't thrilled her sister Ava married a dodgy guy with a criminal past."

Fern sucked in air. "Are you telling me there was a criminal at the McCoy wedding?"

"It's Washington, DC," Leatrice said. "Most of the people here are criminals, if not foreign agents waiting to be activated."

Leatrice saw a conspiracy on every corner and a spy in every coffeeshop. It was why she had a police scanner and a sizable collection of surveillance gear. And it was why I'd given up on keeping things from her.

"You might be right about that." Fern said in a hushed voice, as if we were being listened in on. "I am getting more clients with suspicious accents."

"What's a suspicious accent?" I asked.

"If you ask me, there are people posing as Southerners who do not hail from below the Mason-Dixon," Sidney Allen said in his slow Charleston drawl.

Fern nodded, tapping a finger on his chin. "Very suspicious."

Reese sighed. "Do you know what type of record the brother-in-law has or if he had any issues with the groom?"

"Nope." I took a bite of pizza and chewed slowly. "That would mean I'm investigating, which I'm not."

"If only that was true," Reese said under his breath.

"I told you what I know," I said, ignoring his comment. "Quid pro quo, babe."

"Okay, I'll play." The corners of his mouth quirked up. "Right now, we're trying to establish a timeline and find out if anyone saw anything the morning he vanished. I have officers canvassing the neighborhood to see if anyone can corroborate her story that he left to go on a run at six a.m."

"Where do they live?" Leatrice asked.

"Georgetown," I said. "Just over Wisconsin Avenue a few blocks."

"So, near my salon?" Fern straightened and touched a hand to his hair. "Too bad I'm not in the salon that early or I might have seen something."

"Their street is pretty residential, but I'm sure some neighbors were out and about." I nibbled on the crust of my pizza. "I doubt anyone would have been at the church on the corner, though."

Fern jerked to attention. "Church? Do you mean St. John's?"

"Yes. Why?" I asked.

"One of my shut-in clients lives right near the church."

"I didn't know you had shut-in clients."

He waved a hand at me. "Of course, sweetie. Some of my Georgetown ladies can't get up my steps anymore so I go to them. I set up shop on their kitchen tables and we have a grand old time. Miss Evangeline is one of my favorites. That old girl may not be very mobile anymore, but she doesn't miss a trick. If it happened out her window, she saw it."

"I think I'd like to talk to your client," Reese said.

I thought that I'd like to talk to her, too, but I decided it would be best not to say that out loud.

I nudged Reese. "See how well quid pro quo worked out for you?"

He lowered his mouth so that it tickled my earlobe. "Oh, quid pro quo with you comes much later, babe."

CHAPTER 16

I held my hand up to shield my eyes from the morning sunlight, as I peered up at the soaring columns and wide stone stairs of the Carnegie Institute of Science. Located on 16th Street and a straight shot down from The White House, the massive structure was grand and imposing, and not at all what you imagined when you thought "science institute."

Since it was early in the morning, we'd been lucky enough to find street parking right in front of the building. I hoped Buster and Mack would be as fortunate, although there was a good chance they were riding their Harleys to the walk-through, which would make parking even easier for them.

Kate waved me over to the side of the building. "They don't open the front doors, remember?"

We walked to the side entrance, which was quiet, even though 16th Street was already bustling. Ducking inside the building, we wound our way through the stairs and hallways until we reached the rotunda.

Our shoes echoed on the marble as we crossed the gray and gold starburst pattern of the floor. Tipping my head back, I gazed at the soaring domed ceiling with its ornate skylight and Art Deco chandelier. Gray and ivory marble columns surrounded the circular foyer and were topped with high arches. It wasn't a huge space, but it was striking and made for the perfect ceremony setting. I suspected that even my mother would approve of the grandeur.

"It's not Jamaica, but it's not bad," Mack said, as he and Buster lumbered across the dining room attached to the foyer.

"Thanks for coming," I said as the two burly men in head-to-toe black leather joined us on the marble floor.

Kate shifted her hot-pink Kate Spade purse higher on her shoulder. "I don't know why we needed a walk-through. It's not like we all haven't worked here before."

"It's never a bad idea to do a final walk-through," I said. "Especially since this is so last-minute."

"And especially since Richard insisted on one," Kate added. "Speaking of the darling diva, where is he?"

Richard was almost never late, although to be fair, we were all a few minutes early.

"We can go over all the things that Richard isn't involved in." Buster opened what looked like a leather saddle bag that was slung across his body and pulled out a file folder. "I know you've given us free rein with the design, but do you want the ceremony facing the doors?"

I twisted to take in the space and the soaring iron doors that led out to the front steps, then nodded. "I like the concept of us in the middle and guests seated all around, but the reality of not having a set front and back doesn't appeal."

Kate grinned at me. "Unless you and Reese don't mind pivoting every minute or so during the ceremony."

"Like a rotating restaurant?" I shook my head. "No, thank you."

Mack's pants groaned as he strode to the doors and turned. "So, the aisle will lead to here, and we'll have rows of chairs extending back to the pocket doors."

I nodded. "Cocktails in the library and dinner in the dining room. Long tables."

Buster pivoted to face the rectangular dining room with

two tall windows at one end and a geometric rug covering the hardwood floor. Light spilled in from the windows, but the ceilings were considerably lower than in the attached rotunda. "Naturally. The room was made for long rectangles."

I thought about the reception that was going to be set on the sand in Jamaica, but pushed away the brief pang of regret. There was nothing I could do about a hurricane, and the Carnegie was a beautiful venue. It was just a lot more traditional than I'd imagined my wedding being. I'd also never imagined I'd get married in a place where I'd worked before. Memories of past weddings rushed to my mind, and I gave my head a quick shake, as if to dislodge all the other brides.

"You okay, sweetie?" Mack asked in a low voice as he came up to stand next to me.

I smiled at him. "Totally. It's going to be beautiful."

He eyed me as if he didn't believe my assurance. "It will be, but is it what you want?"

"What I want is to be on a beach with a tropical drink in my hand, but if there's one thing I've learned planning weddings, it's to be flexible." I sighed. "I can control a lot of things, but the weather isn't one of them."

"Isn't that the truth?" He patted my hand with his own beefy one. "Don't you worry. Buster and I will make sure that your day will be extra special."

I leaned into him. Despite his massive size, tattoos, and piercings, he was a big, cuddly teddy bear. "I know you will."

"Sorry we're late!" Richard's voice made us all turn as he and my mother walked across the dining room.

I shot Kate a look, but she shrugged. Clearly, she'd also been unaware that Richard was bringing my mother to the walk-through.

"Annabelle, darling." My mother walked up to me, pulling me into a hug and giving me a quick once-over. "You look a little more rested, although not much. Remind me to give you some of my eye cream before the big day."

I tried to give Richard a look, but he was wisely avoiding my gaze. Why on Earth would he bring my mother to a vendor walk-through where we would discuss load-in times and table placement?

My mother gave Buster and Mack air kisses, asking about Merry and making a thinly veiled comment about how she'd love a grandchild as adorable as their daughter. I ignored all of this and focused my glares on Richard, who was making a point of walking the perimeter of the dining room and taking notes with his back to me.

"Is this where you'll get married?" My mother walked into the rotunda, her pumps tapping the marble like machine gun fire. "Well, it's certainly grand. I suppose if you can't manage to find a church, this is a suitable backup."

Kate's eyebrows rose. I'm sure she'd never heard the stunning historical building referred to as "suitable" before.

Richard plucked a file out of his crossbody bag and flipped it open. "We'll need two sets of chivari chairs. Are we thinking cream?"

"What about natural wood?" I suggested. "With ivory cushions."

My mother crinkled her nose and touched a hand to her brown bob. "That doesn't seem very elegant for a wedding. Don't you want gold?"

I flinched. I wasn't opposed to gold chivari chairs, but I'd had them at probably 80 percent of my weddings in DC. They were very Washington, and the last thing I'd wanted was a typical Washington wedding.

"Gold is always a classic choice." Richard jotted down some notes in his file.

Kate opened her mouth to say something, but I caught her eye and shook my head. She clamped her mouth shut, but she didn't look happy about it.

"An ivory damask tablecloth would look lovely with all this marble," my mother said.

Richard nodded and made more notes. "I have some lovely ivory damasks."

My mouth almost dropped open. If any other client had suggested ivory damask, Richard would be rolling his eyes and making comments about it not being the 1980s anymore. If he agreed to a lace overlay, I was definitely going to break his legs.

Buster and Mack hadn't spoken since Richard had arrived, and I noticed that they weren't taking any notes. Usually, my role was to make sure all the vendors coordinated with each other and were on the same page. In this case, Richard was on his own in wrangling the decor team, and from the looks on their faces, he would not have an easy time of it.

My phone trilled in my pocket and I pulled it out, hoping it was Reese calling to tell me they'd found the groom or cleared the bride. My heart sank a little when I saw Fern's name pop up onto the screen.

"Hey, Fern," I said when I answered, taking a few steps away toward the nearby library to get a little privacy.

"Are you at home?" he asked, his voice a hush.

"At home? No. Why? Are you at my building?"

"Remember the Georgetown lady I told you about? The one who lives near your bride and sees everything?" He took a breath but didn't let me answer. "Well, I'm at her house now, and she has some dirt you're going to want to hear."

CHAPTER 17

"*A*re you sure we should have left your mother at the walk-through?" Kate asked as I drove into Georgetown.

"She's with Richard. She'll be fine."

"It's not her I'm worried about." Kate glanced over at me. "It's your wedding. After all the planning we did in Jamaica, if you end up with gold chivaris and ivory damask..."

"I know, I know." I turned onto the street where our bride lived and slowed down as my SUV began to bounce over the cobblestones and the old streetcar rails embedded in them. "It's not exactly what we had in mind."

"That's an understatement," she muttered. "Frankly, I'm surprised that Richard is going along with all of it. He knows very well what your wedding was going to look like. And he hates ivory damask. He thinks it's one step up from cotton twill."

"I thought that was pin tuck that was one step up from cotton twill."

Kate fluttered a hand in the air. "Six in one half, a dozen in the other."

I decided not to tell Kate that her math—and the expression—weren't quite right. "I'm sure he's trying to help keep the peace with my mother and make her feel important. For some reason, those two really bonded."

"A little too much, if you ask me. Richard is going to have to decide whose best friend he is—yours or your mother's."

The thought of Richard being my mother's best friend sent a shiver down my spine. I loved my mother, but I loved that I'd created a life independent of her in Washington. I was proud of what I'd made for myself in DC, despite her misgivings about me moving to the city and starting my own business. I'd bucked her advice in creating Wedding Belles, ignored her advice on dating, and had assembled a group of friends she would have generously called eclectic. I was happy with my choices, and I did not relish the thought of having her opinion infused into every part of my life again.

I spotted the corner house that Fern had described to me, then wedged my SUV into a tight street space, barely tapping the bumper of the car behind me.

"Totally not hitting," Kate reassured me, as she opened the passenger door. Telling me that none of my bumper taps were considered hits had become part of her job description.

We walked up the crumbling stone steps of the townhouse. It had clearly once been a stunning property, but the black paint on the door was peeling and the wrought iron railings leading to it showed patches of rust. I lifted the brass lion's head door knocker, but before I could bring it down again, the door swung open.

"I saw you from the window." Fern beckoned for us to come inside.

He wore a dark blue suit that looked almost conservative except for the purple paisley ascot puffed up at his neck. I breathed in the scent of high end hair products that seemed to follow Fern as well as the faint smell of dust, as he led us from the dimly lit foyer to the front parlor that boasted a bay window extending toward the street.

A regal woman with snow-white hair sat at a round table

facing outside. Fern's brushes, cans of spray, and heat tools were arranged in front of her.

"Miss Evangeline," Fern said. "These are my friends Annabelle and Kate."

She twisted her head when we approached, holding out a hand. "Fernando's wedding planner friends. It's so lovely to meet you."

"It's nice to meet you," I said taking her hand and shaking it gently.

Kate also shook her hand, grinning at Fern. It was rare we heard anyone call him Fernando, but he seemed unfazed by it and by the fact that his mother had named him after her favorite ABBA song.

"I've heard a lot about you two." Miss Evangeline's soft gray eyes sparkled as she turned to look out her window again. "And all the murders you've solved."

"There haven't been that many." I hoped Fern didn't regale all his clients about his wedding planner friends and all the corpses at their weddings.

"But you have cleared his name before, haven't you?"

"Well, yes," I admitted.

She nodded, as if that was all the answer she needed. "Fernando has been doing my hair for decades. I started using him when his salon was brand new, and no one had any idea who he was."

"That's true." Fern resumed his position behind the woman, gently combing her hair. "Miss Evangeline was one of my very first clients."

"And when I could no longer leave my home, he offered to come to me." She reached a hand back and grabbed one of his. "Isn't that kind of him?"

I knew that, despite his reputation for having glamorous clients and being overly fond of champagne, Fern had a heart of gold and was eternally loyal.

Fern squeezed her thin hand. "I have as much fun as you

do. We watch everyone walk by while I do her hair, and Miss Evangeline knows them all."

She released his hand and tapped a finger to her temple. "When you've lived in the same place for as long as I have, you get to know who comes and goes."

"I'll bet you see a lot." Kate walked to the window and pulled back the sheers that hung over one side of the bay window.

Miss Evangeline nodded. "The neighborhood has changed since I first moved in over forty years ago. Most of the families who were here when I came are gone. Now it's all young couples with fancy jobs who come home late."

I joined Kate at the window. Although there was a space between the window and the sidewalk, it did feel like people were passing right by us. I twisted my neck and saw that Amanda and Brock's house was across from us and only two houses down to the left. "Fern said you noticed something interesting about the couple who live in the pale yellow house across from you. The one with black shutters."

Miss Evangeline's mouth twitched into a smile. "I could write a book about those two, let me tell you."

"Really?" Kate dropped her side of the sheers.

The older woman bobbed her head up and down, and Fern held his comb over her hair, waiting for her to stop moving. "They're one of those I was talking about. Coming and going at all hours."

"That makes sense," I said. "The husband is a television personality."

"Is he?" Miss Evangeline's thin eyebrows arched. "I could see that. He's very handsome."

"He is that," Kate said.

"Did you notice anything recently at their house?" I asked. "Maybe Monday morning?"

The woman tilted her head, pursing her lips as she thought. "Monday morning. It could have been Monday." She gave a small laugh. "Sometimes I forget the days, but now that I think about it, Monday sounds right."

I perched on the bench seat that curved around the bay window. "What happened on Monday?"

Miss Evangeline folded her hands in her lap. "It was early, but I always get up with the birds, so I didn't mind. I was taking my morning tea in here, as usual." She motioned to the window with her head. "I had the curtains drawn, and I saw that good looking young man leave to go on his morning run. He goes out at the same time each morning when it's barely light."

"How did you know it was him?" I asked, noticing that her windows could use a thorough washing.

"He always wears the same thing, although it still strikes me as odd when men wear tights."

"He wore running tights?" I looked out the window toward the house.

"They were black. So was his knitted cap. But his long-sleeved USC T-shirt was burgundy. He always runs in that."

"Always?"

She nodded. "Sometimes it's got short-sleeves, but it's always USC. It must be his alma mater."

I turned back around. "He ran with a cap?"

She nodded. "It's cool when it's that early. Even in July."

I would have to take her word for it. I tried *not* to be out and about before seven in the morning. I leaned back against the bay window. "More confirmation that Brock did go out on his run, like Amanda said."

"That's not the unusual part," Fern said, leaning down close to Miss Evangeline's face. "Tell her the good part, sweetie."

"Oh, yes." Miss Evangeline looked from me to Kate. "Fernando thought you would be interested that I saw a woman that wasn't his wife sneaking up the side of the house to the back entrance. About half an hour after he left."

I sat up straighter, as did Kate.

"How did you know it wasn't his wife?" Kate asked.

"His wife is a pretty thing with dark hair," the woman said. "This one was a blonde."

Kate and I exchanged a look.

"Was her hair short or long?" I asked.

"Long," Miss Evangeline said with a sharp nod.

"Was it very bouncy?" Kate asked. "Or straight?"

"Definitely full. I wish I could have hair with that much get up and go."

Kate's eyes widened as they locked onto mine.

"You could if you'd let me give you a permanent, Miss Evangeline," Fern said.

The woman fluttered a hand at him. "Too much trouble at my age."

I wasn't paying much attention to their conversation, though. There was one person we knew who had hair just like that and who knew the McCoys very well. But why would the bride's sister Ava be sneaking up the side of her sister's house the morning Brock vanished? What was her connection to the disappearance, and did it have anything to do with her husband's criminal past?

CHAPTER 18

"Well, that was interesting," I said, as Kate and I walked down the steps of Miss Evangeline's townhouse.

"You can say that again." Kate clutched the railing, teetering down the steps in her heels which were not made for uneven Georgetown streets. Not that that had ever stopped her before.

We both waved at the bay window and saw the older lady and Fern waving back from where he stood behind her. After watching him comb her hair for a solid fifteen minutes, I suspected his weekly visits were more about conversation than actual hair styling.

"Are you thinking the blonde she saw was Ava?" Kate asked once she'd reached the sidewalk.

"Who else could it be?"

Kate brushed her hands together and small flakes of rust from the railing sifted to the ground. "There are other women with bouncy blond hair in Washington."

"How many of them would be out that early and sneaking up the side of Amanda's house?" I rubbed my arms and noticed that the temperature had dropped a few degrees since we'd been inside and a breeze had picked up, blowing some leaves past us down the brick sidewalk.

Kate frowned. "Miss Evangeline did say sneaking, didn't she?"

"What I don't know is why Amanda's sister would have any reason to be sneaking around the back of the house. I mean, it's her sister and they're close. She would just knock on the front door."

"Or walk in," Kate said. "I'll bet she has a key."

I snapped my fingers. "Excellent point. She probably has a key, so why would she need to sneak in the back? There's nothing back there but a sad excuse for a back yard and a parking space."

"I guess we could always ask Amanda." She nudged me and pointed across the street to where our former bride was getting out of a parked car in front of her house. The brunette had her hair pulled half up and wore a black skirt topped with a black-and white striped T-shirt. She looked better than she had the last time we'd seen her, but considerably more causal than I was used to the former beauty queen looking.

"Why not?" I said under my breath, hurrying across the street and pulling Kate along behind me as she muttered something about not being serious.

Amanda glanced up when we reached her, her eyes widening for a moment before she smiled at us. "Annabelle! Kate! I didn't expect to see you here."

I jerked a thumb behind me. "We happened to be meeting with a new client when we saw you."

She nodded at my explanation. "I guess weddings never stop, do they?"

I didn't answer her question with more than a vague nod. "How are you doing, Amanda?" Although she wasn't wearing as much makeup as she usually did, she was still more made up than I got when I went out to a nightclub, which wasn't often.

She drew in a shaky breath. "Not great. I'm sure you've

heard by now that Brock has been declared missing and the police think—" She slapped a hand across her mouth as her eyes filled with tears.

"I saw." I hadn't seen anything on the news, but I assumed it was all over the media, and I couldn't exactly admit that my fiancé had tipped me off.

She seemed to compose herself after a moment, dropping her hand and nodding. "That morning I called you, I actually thought he might have left me. I knew it was odd of him not to return from his run, but I didn't truly think foul play was involved."

"You were pretty upset," Kate said.

"You would be too if you suspected that your husband of only six months might have walked out on you." Her tone was sharp for a moment, then she seemed to remember herself and modulated her voice. "I was afraid there might be another woman."

"Why would you think that?" I asked.

She shrugged. "He's been distant lately. Besides, women were throwing themselves at him all the time. Even the political types you'd never expect."

"What about Audra Duncan?" Kate asked.

Amanda flinched visibly. "Oh, Brock detests her."

"We heard he got in a fight with her at the station," I said.

"I'm not surprised. He probably got in more than one fight with her." Amanda made a face. "He can't stand that woman."

"So, she wasn't one of the women you suspected he could have been with?" Kate pressed.

I gave her a look, wondering if she just really wanted another reason for Audra to be guilty of something.

"No way." Amanda gave a curt shake of her head. "Honestly, there wasn't anyone that I knew of, and now I guess I was being paranoid and jealous." Her voice cracked. "I suppose I didn't want to deal with the thought of it being something worse than him leaving me."

"And now?" I asked.

She dropped her gaze to the sidewalk. "Now I'm a suspect in my own husband's disappearance, and I have no idea what happened to him or why."

I felt sorry for the woman. She might have been a beauty queen who'd had a lavish wedding to a local celebrity, but right now she was just a grieving wife missing her husband.

"I'm sorry we haven't been able to help more," I said. "We've gone through the list of names you gave us and anyone we could think of, but aside from Audra, none of them seem to have had any altercations with Brock."

She swiped at her eyes, and I was amazed that no mascara came off. Then I reminded myself that she most likely had eyelash extensions. No one had lashes that were naturally that long and dark.

"I appreciate you trying. Honestly, I don't think there's anything else I can do until the police figure out what happened to him." She sighed. "It would be nice if they didn't suspect me, but I guess that's par for the course since I'm his wife."

"It's pretty standard," Kate said. "But if they thought you killed him, they would have arrested you already."

She sucked in a quick breath. "You don't think he's...? They couldn't think I...?"

I narrowed my eyes at Kate before shaking my head vehemently. "Of course not. Kate's just pointing out that the police must not consider you an actual suspect."

"Besides, they have eyewitnesses who saw him leave that morning and the police found his phone on his route," Kate added. "So, it's obvious he went running like you said."

"Right." Amanda looked quizzically at Kate, no doubt wondering how she knew so much about the case.

Before she could ask, I said, "At least you have your sister for moral support. You're lucky she's local."

Amanda's expression changed, and she managed a smile. "I

am. Ava has been amazing. She's actually coming over here soon to keep me company."

"I forget where she lives," I said. "Bethesda?"

"Ballston," Amanda corrected.

"That's even closer. How nice to have family practically next door."

"I'll bet you have keys to each other's places and everything," Kate said.

Amanda gave her another curious look, but nodded. "Sure."

"Annabelle and I have keys to each other's apartments," Kate went on. "We aren't sisters like you and Ava, but after working together for years it feels like we're family."

"I'm sure."

"Is Ava a morning person like Annabelle?" Kate asked, motioning toward me with her head. "This one is always showing up at my place at the crack of dawn."

"Ava?" Amanda actually laughed. "Not exactly. Don't you remember on my wedding day? She was the last bridesmaid to get hair and makeup because she hates waking up early."

"So, she never comes over to your place for early morning coffee?" Kate asked, glancing in the direction of the Potomac River and Ballston on the other side of it. "She's only fifteen minutes away."

"Never," Amanda said.

"When we saw her at your place on Monday, she looked pretty put together," I said.

"I called her an hour before I called you." She frowned. "I don't think she took me all that seriously because she took the time to do her hair and a full face of makeup."

"So, she didn't show up at your place until an hour after you called her?" Kate asked, her mouth gaping slightly.

"At least. Taylor arrived before her. Then again, she lives in Glover Park, so that's not a huge surprise."

I made a mental note that her bridesmaid lived in the

neighborhood just above Georgetown. Not that I thought the dark-haired bridesmaid had anything to do with Brock's disappearance.

"Why are you asking so many questions about Ava?" Amanda asked.

A low rumble of thunder sounded in the distance and we all looked up. The sky had darkened, and it seemed like a summer thunderstorm was about to hit.

"No reason," I said. "It's just nice to have family around when things like this happen."

The wind swirled leaves around our feet as a few fat raindrops splattered the brick sidewalk.

"I'd better get inside," Amanda said, her gaze darting to her townhouse.

I glanced back at my car and saw that Kate was already backing away toward it. "Let us know if you need anything."

She nodded as the rain started coming down harder, and she dashed toward her house. Kate screamed as we darted across the street, the skies opening up and drenching us both as we ran to my car and jumped inside.

When we were both in with the doors closed and the rain hammering the windows, Kate pushed her soaking hair off her face and turned to me. "So, I guess we know that whatever reason Ava had for being at her sister's house that morning, it wasn't something she wanted Amanda to know about."

I shivered and droplets of water dripped onto the floor of my car. "Which means the sister is now suspect number one."

CHAPTER 19

"I'm soaked!" Kate dropped her heels on the rug in my apartment once we'd dripped our way up three flights of stairs.

I was happy to see that no one was home, flicking on the overhead light to illuminate the living room. The thunderstorm had darkened the sky, so no natural light streamed in my windows like it usually did, but the warm glow of the light made it feel cozy.

Kate craned her neck to peer down the hallway that led to the rest of my apartment. "I can't believe your place is empty. It's usually like Grand Central in here."

"Don't remind me," I said, trying to stay on the area rug so I wouldn't drip on my hardwoods. "And don't jinx it."

"I hope Richard and your mother didn't get caught in this." Kate glanced at the windows and the rain coming down in heavy sheets.

"I didn't think you liked my mother."

Kate waved a hand. "Your mother doesn't bother me because she's not *my* mother. I think only our own mother can drive us crazy. And I'm sure a lot of what she does is done out of love, even if it makes you want to pull your hair out."

I was sure Kate was right and wondered when she'd gotten so wise about mothers. "I guess."

"But I do know where you get your iron fist in the velvet glove thing from now."

I opened my mouth to argue, but realized she was probably right about that, too. I had picked up a lot about getting people to do their best work from my mother's Southern belle techniques, although I hated to admit it.

"So, are you going to tell your hot fiancé what we learned about Ava?" Kate asked, letting her purse join her shoes on the floor.

"I hate to rat out the bride's sister, but I can't keep that from him. Not when it's officially a police investigation."

"Good. I hate when we hide things from Reese. He always finds out, anyway."

"I feel bad we haven't done more to help Amanda," I said, shivering a little in my wet clothes.

"Are you kidding? We've already uncovered multiple potential suspects. Sure, Amanda doesn't know about all of them, but I'm sure Reese will be able to clear her name faster with the information we discovered."

"He won't be pleased we interviewed a witness without him."

Kate shrugged. "Maybe not, but he won't be shocked. He knows you, Annabelle. He knows you can't stop yourself if you think you're helping someone. It's one of your most endearing and maddening qualities."

"Thanks, I think."

"You're welcome." She missed my sarcasm entirely. "If you're still in information gathering mode, I think we should go talk to Nikki at the TV station."

"We already talked to her."

"I think there's more she didn't want to say over the phone." Kate winked at me. "Besides, I've always wanted to check out the TV station. And maybe meet a few of the anchors."

"What happened to you wanting to tone down the crazy dating? I thought you'd decided to just date one person."

"I do. I have. But there's no harm in looking." She wagged an eyebrow at me. "For you, too. You're not married yet."

I tried to give her a severe look, but failed and instead shook my head at her.

"You're right," Kate said. "Reese is hotter than any of those stiffs on TV."

I looked down, realizing I'd dripped most of the water from my clothes onto the carpet. I walked quickly down the hall, pulling my wet clothes off as I went and tossing them into the hamper once I'd reached my bedroom. Grabbing a pair of Wedding Belles logo T-shirts, I pulled one over my head and tugged on a pair of jeans. I headed back down the hall with the extra T-shirt in hand, my gaze flitting to the canvas tote bags lining the floor of my home office as I passed the open door.

When I reached the living room, I tossed Kate the dry T-shirt. "You up for some work on my hotel welcome bags?"

"I'd forgotten about those." She eyed the shirt with our company logo on the front in gold. "Do they even make sense anymore?"

I popped into the kitchen while Kate peeled off her top and replaced it with the company shirt. It was too early to pour a glass of wine, so I retrieved two sodas from the fridge and headed toward my office. "Not really, but there's no time to order different things for the bags."

Since my wedding was supposed to be in the Caribbean, the hotel welcome bags for my wedding were canvas beach bags stuffed with mini tubes of sunscreen, bug repellent wipes, bottles of jerk sauce, banana chips, and tropical-scented travel candles. Not exactly items you'd need for a wedding in the nation's capital.

Kate joined me to stand in the doorway to the office. "It's

not really a big deal. Everyone gets that you had to scramble at the last minute to reschedule. It will be like an inside joke to get a bottle of jerk sauce when you're staying at the Marriott in DC."

"Just what I always wanted." I sighed as I surveyed the tropical colors of the items to be stuffed in the bags. "A joke wedding."

Kate threw one arm around my shoulders. "I promise you that your wedding will not be a joke."

"Yoo hoo!" The familiar warbling voice drifted down the hall from my front door.

Kate sighed. "I cannot promise that it won't be filled with crazies, though."

Leatrice hurried down the hall toward us in a garishly colored, floral print Muumuu that almost covered the red rain boots decorated with images of chickens. Hermès was tucked under one arm, but he wasn't wearing a Muumuu or rain boots, which was a bit of a surprise. "I'm so glad you're back." She eyed us up and down. "You two look like a pair of drowned rats, but the shirts are cute."

"Thanks." I glanced at her outfit, but I'd learned not to ask about her wardrobe choices. I was just glad the dog wasn't dressed up. "Is everything okay?"

"If you consider a drug conviction okay," she said, putting Hermès on the floor.

Kate and I exchanged a look, then Kate gave her head a shake. "I'm sorry. Who are we talking about again?"

"Sorry." Leatrice giggled. "You remember the brother-in-law you mentioned last night? The one with the criminal record?"

"Yes," I said slowly. "But I didn't mention his name."

Leatrice flapped a bony hand at me. "I knew the name of the missing TV fellow and it was easy enough to search up his wife's maiden name, her sister and then the sister's husband's name."

"Please tell me you weren't on the dark web again." I rubbed a hand across my forehead.

"Don't be silly, dear." Leatrice patted my arm. "I never go on there anymore. Boots and Dapper Dan do all my searches for me."

I groaned to myself. I was definitely not going to tell Reese that Leatrice was still in contact with hackers who frequented the dark web. Some things it was better he *didn't* know.

"So, you found out that the brother-in-law was arrested on drug charges?" Kate asked as Hermès circled her feet and then bounded into my office, scampering around the bags and boxes.

Leatrice nodded. "Yes, but it looks like a lot of the charges were dropped because he made a deal. And the way he's mentioned in the reports and the fact that some of the information is sealed makes me think that he might still be working as a CI."

Kate tilted her head at the woman. "CI?"

"Confidential informant, dear," Leatrice said, looking at Kate like she was a simpleton. "Don't you remember from our missing Santa case?"

I wouldn't have termed it *our* missing Santa case, but Leatrice did help us with an investigation the previous Christmas.

"So, the brother-in-law might still be involved with some sort of criminal element?" I ran a hand though my wet hair. "I wonder if that could have anything to do with Brock's disappearance."

"If it does, there's way more going on than we know about," Kate said. "And why would being related to a CI put you in danger? I doubt the two men were connected except for their wives. Although if the brother-in-law was involved it might explain the sister's odd behavior."

"Odd behavior?" Leatrice visibly perked up.

I gave Kate an almost imperceptible shake of my head. The

more Leatrice knew, the wilder her conspiracy theories usually became. With everything already going on, I really couldn't handle Leatrice deciding to stake out the brother-in-law.

Before Kate or I could try to talk our way out of it, there was a commotion at the door. My stomach tightened as I recognized Richard's voice — and my mother's.

CHAPTER 20

"So, we're all having dinner together?" I asked, as Richard hoisted several sacks of groceries onto my kitchen counters. "Here?"

I peeked over the counter and through the opening between my kitchen and living room to where Kate, Leatrice, and my mother were sitting. The conversation was low enough that I couldn't hear what they were saying. I could only hope Leatrice wasn't talking about the dark web or her hacker buddies. My mother already thought my living in the city was dangerous. If she knew that my downstairs neighbor kept a police scanner and regularly followed people she suspected of being spies, she would be convinced that I lived in a crime hot spot.

"Yes, Annabelle." He gave me a withering look. "Would you rather we all go out in this monsoon?"

I wouldn't have called it a monsoon, and I could already hear that the rain was slacking off. "A little advance notice would have been nice."

"I did call you, but you didn't answer."

"Good news about the hotel welcome bags," Kate said as she joined us, her voice unnaturally bright. "Your mother and

Leatrice are going to get some more DC-themed things to put in them tomorrow."

"My mother?" I glanced at the living room. "And Leatrice? Together?"

Kate spread her arms open wide. "Believe me, it was not my suggestion. But one thing led to another and…"

"Well, that should be interesting," Richard said. "Does Leatrice still wear goggles when she drives?"

"Not always." I felt the need to defend her, although her vintage Ford Fairmont made enough of a statement that it didn't matter what Leatrice wore when she drove it. The fact that she usually sat on some old phone books to see over the enormous steering wheel and occasionally wore an aviator scarf was almost beside the point. "And the goggles come in handy when the AC is on the fritz and she drives with the windows open."

Richard folded the paper bags flat onto the counter and surveyed his supplies. "Like I said, interesting."

I thought about my well-heeled and well-dressed mother tooling around in a sedan from the 1980s that was almost as long as some limousines. Well, she'd wanted to be involved. Driving with Leatrice was definitely a trial by fire that we'd all experienced.

The door to my apartment opened and from both the excited voices from the living room, I knew it had to be my fiancé. Only Reese got that reaction from Leatrice and my mother.

"Hey, babe." He poked his head into the kitchen. "Are we having a party I didn't know about?"

I jerked a thumb at Richard. "Ask him."

"I'm cooking dinner," Richard said, taking an onion from a mesh bag. "I thought my food would be a step up from your usual takeout."

Reese came into the room and wrapped his arms around me from behind. "How's the bride?"

For a moment I thought he meant Amanda, then I realized he was talking about me because our wedding was in a few days. "I'm fine."

"How was the walk-through?"

I was impressed he'd remembered about it since he'd dashed out so quickly in the morning. Then again, as a detective he was used to remembering details, and he did seem to retain things I said, even when I thought he wasn't listening. "It was okay."

"If you like ivory damask," Kate muttered.

Richard pressed his lips together as he pulled a knife out of a drawer. "You know as well as I do that the Carnegie is classic DC. Ivory looks lovely in the dining room."

Kate pretended like she was snoring and lolled her head to one side. "Oh, I'm sorry. I must have nodded off because damask linens are so boring."

Richard's cheeks flushed, and he twisted to face us. "What did you want me to do?"

Kate put her hands on her hips. "Maybe take Annabelle's side? She's the bride and the client. And she's the one who's supposed to be your best friend, isn't she?"

Richard's mouth fell open, and his gaze went to me. "Is this what you think? That I wasn't taking your side?"

"That's what it felt like," I said. "I appreciate you taking on so much of the planning now that we've had to move the wedding to DC, and I'm grateful you've entertained my mother, but it feels like my wedding is becoming about someone else."

Reese had stilled behind me, and even though I could still hear my mother and Leatrice gabbing in the next room, the kitchen had gone quiet.

Richard blinked a few times. "You're right. I lost track of who my client is." He gave himself a small shake. "But in my defense, your mother can be very persuasive."

"Tell me about it," I muttered.

"Does this mean we can lose the ivory linens?" Kate asked.

Richard turned back to his onion. "Of course. But if you want to keep your wedding out of your mother's hands, you're going to need to put someone else on her. I can't seem to say no to a Southern mother of the bride."

"Well, she's spending tomorrow with Leatrice," Kate said. "If the two of them hit it off, maybe Leatrice can keep her busy for the rest of the week."

I hated to imagine the ways in which Leatrice would amuse my mother. I twisted my head to look up at Reese. "What are your plans for the next few days?"

"Aside from working the Brock McCoy case and my bachelor party tomorrow night?"

"Bachelor party?" Richard's head snapped up. "I didn't know about a bachelor party."

The faintest hint of pink tinged my fiancé's cheeks. "It's something my brother is throwing together with some of the guys from the station. You're welcome to join us."

Richard hesitated. "Since I'm both the Man of Honor and a groomsman, I probably should attend."

Kate's eyebrows rose, and I knew she was thinking what I was. It was hard to imagine Richard hanging out with a bunch of cops. Then again, he would be the perfect spy on the inside.

"You should go," I said. If Richard attended, nothing too crazy would happen because Reese would know it would get right back to me.

"Really?" Richard and Reese asked at the same time.

I nodded. "You *are* a groomsman."

"And the Man of Honor," Richard added with a self-satisfied sniff.

"Even more reason," I said.

"Very well." Richard sighed, as if attending the party was a major sacrifice. "What's the attire?"

"Cop casual."

Richard crinkled his nose. "Isn't that redundant?"

I peered up at my fiancé as Richard muttered about having to buy an outfit so he could slum it. "I thought you only had to work half a week?"

"The McCoy case is a big one, babe. He's a big name—at least locally. And so far, we don't have much to go on."

I turned to face him, his arms still looped around my waist. "Then wait until you hear what we found out."

His expression went from amused to serious as Kate and I took turns telling him what we'd learned about Brock McCoy's sister-in-law creeping around the house the morning he disappeared and then what Leatrice had learned about the brother-in-law's past.

"I'll look into the CI files," he said once we'd finished. "I doubt an old drug case would have anything to do with a political pundit vanishing, but it's worth checking out. Should I ask how Leatrice came about this information?"

"Definitely not," I said.

"What do you think about the neighbor seeing Amanda's sister?" Kate asked.

"I'd like to talk to the neighbor first. You said she saw this from inside her house, right? And she's elderly? It's not that I don't believe her, but eyewitness accounts are notoriously flawed. She might have seen someone, but I don't want to jump to any conclusions about the sister-in-law. So far, we don't have any reason to suspect she had anything to do with the death."

I felt slightly deflated that Reese didn't think the clue was as huge as Kate and I had, but I also knew he was a detective and had to be overly cautious. I guessed he was right. We didn't know for sure Miss Evangeline had seen Ava. We'd assumed it was her since she fit the description, but it was a big leap to make her an automatic suspect. Especially since she didn't have any motive that we knew of.

"Wait a second." I peered up at Reese. "Did you say death?"

"Did you find a body?" Kate asked, her voice low and her eyes wide.

"Not exactly." Reese let out a breath. "But we did find a phone holder you wear around your arm when you run. It was not far from where we located his phone. Brock McCoy's wife confirmed that he used one that was the same make and color."

"Why would that mean he was killed?" I asked, goosebumps prickling my arms.

"Because it was covered in his blood."

CHAPTER 21

"You're sure about this?" Kate asked the next day as she pulled into a parking space in front of the TV studio. "You wouldn't rather be out shopping with Leatrice and your mother?"

I saw that a grin was teasing her mouth as she said this. "Not by a long shot." Even though dinner the night before had ended up being pleasant—helped along by Richard's excellent seared salmon in a tomato spinach cream sauce—I was glad for a break from both Leatrice and my mother.

I wasn't sure how I felt about the fact that the two seemed to get along so well. I didn't remember them hitting it off when my mother had attended my engagement party. Then again, Leatrice was someone that it could take a while to warm up to. She'd tried to set me up with every UPS and pizza delivery guy who entered our building for a year before we became friendly—and before I found out why I got such strange looks when I signed for packages or pizza.

"It's nice to have a break from thinking about the wedding," I said as we got out of the car. "But I can't help feeling I should be doing more. We're sure everything is under control?"

"Absolutely." Kate tugged at her snug black pencil skirt

and readjusted her blouse so that more of her cleavage showed. "I confirmed with our new hotel blocks and turned in final numbers. Richard is on top of the catering, Buster and Mack are handling all the decor, and your hot fiancé is picking up the marriage license."

The marriage license!" I slapped my forehead. "Wasn't Fern doing that?"

"Don't worry." She hooked her arm through mine as we walked toward the front door of the concrete building. "Fern submitted the application, but he couldn't get away from his salon to pick it up, so I put Reese on it. Besides, he probably has friends down at the courthouse. It'll be easy for him."

"Thanks." Anything that would save me the hassle of trudging through the DC courthouse to wait at the marriage bureau.

"Hey, you're the bride." She slid her sunglasses from her face to the top of her head, as we stepped through the glass double doors and into the lobby of the TV station.

A cool blast of air conditioning in the building's foyer made me glad I'd worn my blue wrap dress with sleeves. We signed in at the front desk, clipping visitor badges onto our lapels, and were waved into the main part of the station. Luckily, our makeup artist friend Nikki had put our names on the approved guest list, so we had no trouble getting in and moving about freely.

"Do you think Brock had an office?" I whispered as we walked down a hallway with door after door boasting brass nameplates.

"If he did, I don't see it." She made a face. "Unless they've already taken his name off."

I shivered, and not because of the frigid air. "That's morbid. I doubt they'd move on so quickly. It's only been a few days."

Kate shrugged. "Show biz is brutal."

We came to the end of the hallway and an open door.

Looking in, I saw a wall of mirrors and several stools positioned down the length of it.

"There are my favorite wedding planners!" The African-American woman with a glossy, black pixie cut and perfect makeup rushed over to give us hugs.

"Hey, Nikki." Kate exchanged air kisses with her.

Nikki appraised my assistant's face and nodded. "Looking good, girl. Are you using that setting spray I told you to?"

"Of course," Kate said. "From your lips to Sephora's shopping bag."

Nikki laughed, then pivoted to me and gave me a quick hug. "Annabelle. Still rocking the natural look, eh?"

I didn't consider foundation, powder, mascara, and lipstick the natural look, but I guessed compared to her stunning smoky eye look, I was pretty bare bones.

"She's saving the big guns for her wedding day," Kate said, waving a hand at my face. "She's even going to let you do falsies on her."

"Falsies?" I glanced down at my chest.

"Your lashes, girl." Nikki laughed again. "I'm going to give you dramatic eyes for your wedding day."

Flying a makeup artist down to Jamaica hadn't been in the budget, but now that we were local, Kate had booked Nikki to do my wedding day makeup. I was both excited and slightly terrified to see how glamorous she would make me. Part of me was afraid that Reese wouldn't recognize me coming down the aisle.

"Thanks for letting us visit you at the studio." Kate spun around and took in the room. "I guess you're between shows now."

Nikki nodded as she walked back to her chair and waved for us to follow. "Most of the action happens early in the morning, a little before noon, and then right before five o'clock."

I didn't watch a lot of news or political shows, but I tried to think of some of the faces on the network shows. "Do you do Courtney Brandt? She always looks great."

Nikki beamed. "She's a sweetheart."

Kate glanced over her shoulder and dropped her voice. "So, spill the tea. Who's awful to work on?"

Nikki nibbled the edge of her bottom lip. "Everyone's great."

Clearly, a lie. Not that I blamed her.

"You told us that Brock McCoy is nice to work with, right?" I asked.

Her face relaxed. "Brock's easy. He's so good looking, I don't need to do much. Not like some of others who need me to contour them to death just so their nose doesn't take up half the screen."

Kate snorted a laugh.

"Is there anyone here who doesn't like Brock?" I asked.

Nikki tilted her head at me. "Why? Does this have to do with him being missing?"

"We promised Amanda we'd ask around for her," I said. "See who might have had a problem with him."

Nikki rested one hand on the back on the nearest canvas backed stool. "I'd say it was the opposite, actually. Everyone loved Brock. He's got this magnetic personality that seems to draw people to him." She paused and gave us a knowing look. "Especially women."

"Not surprising, considering how attractive the guy is," Kate said. "Of course, Audra Duncan isn't charmed by him. You told us that yourself."

"Her." Nikki wrinkled her nose in obvious disgust. "She's one face I'd be happy never to touch again."

I noticed that Kate looked pleased by this news. "I don't blame you. That woman is a terror."

"How do you know her?" Nikki asked.

Kate shook her head. "Long story and better over cocktails."

"Did you overhear Audra and Brock arguing often?" I asked, trying to steer the conversation back to our former groom. "Aside from the fight you told us about last week."

"Oh, sure. Those two went at it all the time. If they weren't fighting over politics, they were sniping at each other over stupid stuff."

"Really?" Kate crossed her arms over her chest. "So, they didn't only fight over political opinions?"

"I wish." Nikki blinked her impossibly lush lashes a few times. "Those two argued about anything and everything."

"Well, that's not good," Kate said.

"What do you mean?" I asked. "We already knew about Audra."

"Men and women don't fight that much unless there's passion."

I usually trusted Kate's expertise when it came to relationships, especially the tawdry kind. "You're saying they were having an affair?"

Kate held up her hands, palms facing out. "I'm not saying I know for a fact, but couples who fight usually have something going on. I would have had to see them together to know for sure."

Nikki nodded slowly. "Come to think of it, that would not surprise me. I love Brock, but the guy isn't the most discreet about his flirtations, if that's what they are."

"If they were involved, that would definitely give Audra a motive," I said. "So, was there anyone else he fought with?"

"As in an actual screaming fight like the ones he had with Audra?" Nikki frowned as she thought. "No, but he did have a guy thrown out of the station last week."

"An aggressive fan?" Kate asked.

"Nope. Apparently, his brother-in-law."

My mouth went dry. "Did you say his brother-in-law?"

Nikki nodded. "That's what he said after he had the guy removed. That he couldn't believe his wife's sister had married a guy like that. I remember he called his wife right afterward and was telling her all about it. Said the jerk was trying to extort him, and she needed to be careful. Then he told her he'd take care of it." Nikki gave an embarrassed laugh. "People say all sorts of things in front of me when they're in my chair."

"Wow," Kate said. "That's crazy."

I agreed. I wondered what Brock had meant when he said he'd take care of it. Had trying to take care of his brother-in-law ended up badly for him?

"I think I need to call my fiancé," I said.

"Who is your fiancé?" The sharp voice made us all swing our heads to the open door. A young woman with pale hair slicked into a tight, high bun stood with her arms crossed.

I didn't have time to ask who she was before she strode forward, extending a business card to me. "I'm Teegan Thomas, Mr. McCoy's publicist."

I vaguely remembered Nikki mentioning Brock's publicist —and that she was intense. I glanced down at the ivory business card she put in my hand. It looked like she owned her own PR firm, even though she didn't look over twenty-five.

"Who are you?" She shot a quick glare at Nikki then returned her steely gaze to me and Kate.

"We planned Brock's wedding," I said, hoping that would gain us some favor.

She nodded, her lips pressed together in a white line. "Amanda mentioned that she'd spoken to you. A mistake on her part, but one I hope to fix."

Nikki took a step back, and I didn't blame her. This woman might be young, but she was tough.

"We're only trying to help," Kate said.

"I've read all the media write-ups about you. Your clients rarely benefit from your 'help.'" She used air quotes on the last word.

I was trying hard not to be offended, but I really wanted to slap the smug expression off her face. "We have a pretty high success rate. We'll find out what happened to Brock. Unless maybe you're worried about that. You wouldn't happen to be hiding anything the police would be interested in, would you?"

She blanched, but recovered quickly. "Stay away from my clients."

"I didn't know Amanda was your client," Kate said.

Teegan Thomas shifted her deadly gaze from me to Kate and back. "She is now." She turned on her heel and stalked out of the room.

"I should have warned you about her," Nikki said. "She's been hanging around the station ever since Brock disappeared."

Kate made a face. "Talk about a dedicated publicist."

"A little too dedicated, if you ask me." I stared at the door she'd disappeared through. "She's clearly terrified about us finding out something."

CHAPTER 22

"*B*abe," Reese said when he finally picked up his phone line at the police station. He sounded out of breath and a little impatient, which was unusual for him.

"Sorry to bother you at work." Even though we were driving near the District Two station on our way back from the TV station, I'd decided not to pop in on my future husband unannounced. I'd done it before with mixed results.

He let out a breath. "No, it's not you. It's this case."

"Brock McCoy?"

Kate glanced over at me as we idled at a red light, mouthing the word *What?*

I put a finger to my lips, as I let Reese talk.

"We're getting lots of calls on the tip line, but most are bogus," he said. "I know we can place him leaving his house in Georgetown, but we don't have anyone who can place him on the trail. No one has called in to report seeing a man being attacked or taken. I know it was early in the morning, but someone had to have seen something. That phone didn't materialize on the path by itself."

"Considering the fact that everyone records their lives on their phones, I'm shocked no one has video of him from that

morning." I shifted my phone to my other ear as Kate accelerated the car. "What about cameras along the path?"

My fiancé blew out another loud breath. "The spot where
the phone was dropped doesn't have coverage. We're pulling
footage from as many stores in Georgetown as possible, but not
all of them are functional. The ones that are show him running
with his head down and that's it. Once he gets to that dead
section of the path, we lose him entirely. So far, it's like the guy
left Georgetown and vanished into thin air."

"You'll find him," I said, bracing one hand against the dashboard as Kate took a sharp turn. "You always do."

"Thanks, babe. I don't mean to unload on you. It's just that
there's a lot of pressure from my captain, and I thought I
would have been sitting on a beach with you by now instead of
sitting at my crappy desk and sifting through grainy footage
that tells me nothing."

With all the drama I'd been dealing with, it was easy for me
to forget that this was his wedding, too. We'd both wanted a
low-key wedding on the sand and now that wasn't happening.
"I know. It completely sucks. I wish we were in Jamaica
tossing back fruity drinks with paper umbrellas instead of here
talking about a missing political pundit. Want me to whip up
some rum punch for us when I get home? I could sneak some
down to the station for you."

He let out a laugh. "That sounds great, but I'm not sure if
drinking this early in the day would be a good idea."

"You do know that Leatrice and my mother are out shopping together, right?"

"Scratch that. We should have started drinking hours ago."

"We can always have a drink tonight," I told him, dropping
my voice even though Kate was right beside me. "A private
happy hour."

He groaned. "Tonight is my pseudo bachelor party."

My heart sank a little. "That's right. I'd forgotten it's
Thursday already."

"I would cancel it if my brother— "

"Don't be silly," I said quickly. "Daniel planned it and you should go." No way was I going to be one of those controlling and jealous wives, especially since we weren't even married yet. "Besides, Richard would be heartbroken if you cancelled it."

Reese choked back a laugh. "I'm sure he would." There was a low murmur of voices in the background. "Well, I'd better run, babe."

"Wait, I haven't told you why I called."

"It wasn't just so I could hear your lovely voice?" he teased.

"No." My face warmed. Even though we lived together and were getting married, his flirting still made me blush. "Kate and I dug up a clue about Brock and his brother-in-law."

"Darren Spencer?"

"Is that his name?" I put my hand over the mouthpiece and turned to Kate. "Did you know that the brother-in-law's name is Darren Spencer?"

Kate shook her head. "Doesn't ring a bell. He wasn't in Amanda and Brock's wedding party, so I don't think I ever heard it."

Now that she mentioned it, I recalled that Ava's husband had been on the outskirts of the activity at her sister's wedding. I vaguely remembered that he was decent looking, but not nearly as striking at Brock.

"So, what did you find out?" Reese asked.

"According to our makeup artist friend who overheard a lot at the TV station where Brock works, Darren was trying to extort him. He showed up at Brock's work and was removed from the station by security."

"Extort him? For what?"

"That she didn't know, but Brock discussed the incident with his wife."

"She didn't mention a word of this when we questioned her."

"Maybe she didn't want to implicate her sister's husband," I said, air-braking on the passenger's side as Kate barely missed the car in front of us.

"Between her sister possibly sneaking around her house and her brother-in-law trying to extort her husband, it looks like they had more family troubles than Amanda wanted to let on." Reese cleared his throat. "Listen babe, I appreciate you and Kate getting this information, but shouldn't you be focused on our wedding?"

"Shouldn't you?" I shot back, regretting my words the moment I said them.

"Maybe," he said, his voice measured. "But this bride isn't even your client anymore and we have half the department working on the case. I think you can take a break this one time."

Now I let out a long breath. "Maybe you're right. I did just get warned off by Brock's attack dog publicist. I think I've been welcoming the distraction, so I don't have to think about how our wedding is going to be nothing like we'd planned."

"Even if we aren't going to be barefoot in the sand, we're still getting married, remember?" Reese's deep voice was soft. "Isn't that the whole point?"

"I can't believe you quoted me back to me." I was always reminding my couples not to lose focus on the entire point of wedding planning, which was the marriage, not the big party.

"I learned from the best."

"Kiss ass," I muttered, hearing his low chuckle in response.

"I have to go, babe," he said. "But I'll see you later tonight." He paused. "I love you, Annabelle Archer."

Now my cheeks really burned. "I love you, too, Michael Reese."

That earned me another low laugh before the phone clicked off. When I dropped it back in my purse and looked at Kate, she was fanning herself with one hand as she steered the car through Georgetown with the other.

"Sometimes you and sexy cop are so hot."

I swatted her arm. "Stop it."

"And you're blushing." She put both hands back on the steering wheel as she attempted to park the car nose first in a parallel spot in front of my apartment building. "It's really cute that he can still make you blush. You know, I give you two better than average odds."

"Thanks." Kate and I sometimes placed bets on how long a couple would last, but it had never occurred to me that she'd be placing odds on my marriage to Reese.

"Anytime." She grinned at me. "So, what did he think about our clue?"

"He thinks that Amanda has a pretty dysfunctional family and that I should pay more attention to our wedding and less to his case."

"That sounds familiar." She turned off the ignition even though the back of her car wasn't completely in the parking space. "But when have you ever taken that advice?"

"We haven't been actively hunting down clues," I argued. "Not like we have in the past, at least."

"True. But there also isn't a dead body." She reached back and grabbed her purse out of the back seat. "If there was a dead body, you'd be all over clues and suspects like wild rice."

"I think you mean, like white on rice."

She tilted her head at me, her brow furrowed. "That doesn't sound right."

Kate didn't mangle expressions as badly as she used to, but I also was so used to them that I didn't notice her malaprops quite so much. My fear was that one day her garbled versions would sound normal to me.

"I do want to know why that publicist was so worked up about us," I said.

"Jealousy? You know how many people claim they want to be wedding planners."

I could imagine Teegan Thomas barking orders at a

wedding party. "Doubtful. I think that woman is in the right business."

"Well, she has her hands full now. The story of Brock McCoy being missing is all over the media."

"So much for Amanda avoiding bad publicity." I felt a pang of regret for my client.

We both got out of the car and headed for my stone-fronted apartment building. After pushing open the front door, we slipped off our shoes out of habit. Even though Leatrice was probably still out with my mother, I didn't want to take any chances.

Once we were halfway up the three flights, Kate whispered, "Are you and Reese really upset you're not getting married on the beach?"

I shrugged, not wanting to lie but knowing there was nothing Kate could do about it. "We'll get over it. Besides, I'm sure Carnegie will be lovely."

Kate didn't reply as we reached my apartment, and I opened the door. For a moment, neither of us could say anything as we stared at the scene in my living room.

"What do you think?" my mother asked from the couch where she and Leatrice sat surrounded by so many shopping bags and boxes that I could barely make out the floor. On the coffee table were what looked like at least two open bottles of wine.

"Hurricane Dolly has nothing on your mother," Kate said under her breath.

CHAPTER 23

"What is all this?" I asked, stepping gingerly over a bag overflowing with bags of Old Bay seasoned potato chips.

"We bought out the city," my mother said, flopping back on the couch, her smile unusually wide.

"I can see that." I peered inside one bag and saw it stacked to the brim with individual cupcake boxes from Baked and Wired. There were several boxes filled with bottles of Fiji water and postcards of cityscapes were strewn across the coffee table. A pile of DC city guides sat between my mother and Leatrice, and it looked like they'd dragged all the canvas tote bags out of my office and arranged them at their feet.

"Your friend here knows a lot about the city." My mother patted Leatrice on the leg. "And a lot about what you and Michael enjoy."

Leatrice beamed at the compliment. "I've been watching her bring boxes of cupcakes home for years."

Kate choked back a snort of laughter.

"I do love Baked and Wired." I could smell the heady scent of sugar wafting up from the cupcake boxes, and my stomach growled in response.

"We thought we should keep the tropical items." My

mother waved to the bags on the floor. "As a nod to the wedding you were supposed to have. But we have lots of DC themed goodies to add to it."

"It actually looks great," I said.

"And smells even better," Kate eyed the cupcakes. "I'm starving."

My mother raised a hand over her head and flapped it toward my kitchen. "We also stocked your refrigerator. You didn't have anything at all in there, Annabelle. I don't know how you feed a big strapping man like Michael with the sad excuse for food in your kitchen."

I didn't answer, knowing that explaining to my mother that I worked for a living and didn't have time to cook every night would be pointless.

"I told her that you two like takeout," Leatrice said in a conspiratorial whisper.

"Thanks" I tried not to bristle at my mother making a face.

"Once we get these finished, we can deliver them to the hotels," Leatrice said.

"Are you sure?" I asked. Usually delivering bags was something Kate and I did, not that it was a task I relished.

Leatrice bobbed her head up and down. "My Sidney Allen is busy with an event tonight, so your mother and I are going to drop off the bags and then hit the town."

"Hit the town?" I stared at them both.

"Don't look so shocked, Annabelle," my mother said, patting her brown bob. "I know how to cut loose."

The idea of my mother and Leatrice cutting loose was something I really didn't want to think about.

"Where are you going?" Kate asked, perching on the arm of the nearest chair.

"Dinner at The Graham Hotel," my mother said.

"And then cocktails at one of the unmarked speakeasies," Leatrice added. "We might hit a few of them if we have time."

"You know about the hidden speakeasies?" Kate gaped at Leatrice.

"Of course, dear." My neighbor shook her head at Kate. "My Honeybun knows all the best spots in the city."

Somehow I had a hard time imagining the roly-poly entertainment diva bellying up to the secret bars in the city and ordering a Sidecar, but I guess I didn't know her husband as well as I thought I did.

"Wow." Kate turned to me. "Your mother's been here for a couple of day and already her social life is more exciting than yours."

I spared Kate a withering look before turning back to Leatrice. "If you're bar hopping, I guess you aren't driving."

My mother held up her phone. "I have Lyft."

"You use Lyft?" I asked. "Are you sure this is a good idea?"

My mother laughed. "We'll be fine. You can follow us on Twitter if you want to know where we are."

I wasn't sure what was happening. My mother knew about Junior League and St. John, not Lyft and Twitter.

I looked at Kate, who just shrugged. "Hey, as long as they're delivering the hotel welcome bags for us, I'm fine with it."

"You're welcome to join us," Leatrice said.

"We can't," Kate said before I could answer. "We have plans."

I lowered my voice. "We do?"

"Your bachelorette party," Kate whispered. "Don't you remember Fern said he was planning it?"

"I thought he was joking about that. It's not a booze cruise, is it?"

She shook her head. "I actually don't know the details."

"Who's coming?" I asked. "Richard is tied up at Reese's bachelor party."

Before she could tell me, the door swung open and Fern flounced into the room. A few feet, at least, until he hit the wall of bags and boxes. He unleashed a torrent of air kisses and finger waves at Leatrice and my mother.

He scanned me and Kate, frowning. "You aren't wearing that, are you?"

I glanced down at my cotton wrap dress and suspected it was not what he considered appropriate bachelorette attire. "I just found out about the party, so I hadn't planned on wearing this out."

Fern's gaze slid to Kate. "You forgot to tell her?"

She twitched one shoulder up. "It's been a little hectic lately."

"No matter." He fluttered a hand in the air. "We have time. They aren't meeting us for another hour at least."

"Who's meeting us?" I asked.

He put a finger over his lips, winking at me. "As if I would spoil the surprise, sweetie. Now run along and change."

"Into what?" I asked as I headed down the hallway toward my bedroom.

"Something sexy," he called out.

Kate's heels tapped rapidly behind me, and I turned to see her following me.

"You're leaving Fern with them?" I asked, jerking a thumb behind us to where Leatrice and my mother were sitting.

Kate winked at me. "Your mother might benefit from one of Fern's style enhancements."

The last time Fern had enhanced someone's style, Leatrice had gone from brunette to platinum blond.

"Besides, I think you need my help," she said. "Your closet is not filled with sexy options."

"Not all of us try to pick up groomsmen every weekend," I muttered as we walked into my bedroom, and she headed for my walk-in closet.

I kicked off my shoes, as I heard her sliding hangers and pawing through clothes.

"Try this." She tossed out a red dress I didn't know I had and wasn't sure I'd ever worn.

I took off my wrap dress and tossed it on my bed before pulling the red jersey dress over my head and shimmying it down my hips.

Kate's phone trilled, and she answered it as she continued to rummage through my clothes. Her voice was muffled behind the closet door, so I mostly heard mumbled yeses and a few excited thank you's.

I tugged the high hemline of the dress, peering at my reflection in the full-length mirror on the back of my bedroom door. Although the dress was snug-fitting, the ruching down the side made it less revealing. I turned to the side and sucked in my stomach. Normally I didn't wear red because of my auburn hair, but this dress didn't look half bad.

Kate stepped out of the closet. "You're not going to believe —" She stopped when she saw me, giving me the once-over. "Now, that is hot."

"You think?" I tugged at the hem again. "It's not too short? Or too red?"

She nodded. "It's perfect. And it's your bachelorette party, not a bridal tea."

She had a point. "What were you saying when you walked out? What was I not going to believe?"

"Right." She snapped her fingers. "That was Nikki on the phone. She recommended us for an upcoming bridal segment for the morning show."

"Really? That's awesome." I put my hands on my hips. "Why wouldn't I believe that?"

"Get this. She said the last wedding planner they had on was a disaster because she caused a bunch of drama at the station by flirting with the on-air talent."

"That's not good. Who would do that?" As soon as the words were out of my mouth, I knew.

"Yep," Kate said. "Brianna."

Despite the owner of Brides by Brianna being a wedding planner, I would never trust her around an eligible—or ineligible—bachelor. The first time I'd met Brianna, she'd practically thrown herself at Reese. "Why am I not surprised?"

"And guess which married man she was flirting with so much that they banned her from the station?" Kate cocked an eyebrow.

"Please don't say Brock McCoy."

She nodded slowly. "The one and only. Apparently, Teegan Thomas went ballistic on her. Threatened to ruin her and threatened to kill her if she came near her client again."

CHAPTER 24

"This is *not* on our way." Fern peered out the window of our Lyft as we drove out of Georgetown toward the heart of the city. Even though it was early evening, the summer sun hadn't set, and the streets were busy with rush hour traffic.

"It's not far out of the way," Kate corrected, leaning forward from the middle of the sedan's back seat and poking her head next to the driver. "One stop at The Hay-Adams Hotel across from the White House."

"Remind me again why we're stopping at a hotel bar on the way to my surprise bachelorette party." I tugged at my dress, which had slid dangerously high up on my thighs. I'd have to remember not to sit down for the rest of the evening.

"You know the Thursday Therapy wedding planner happy hour is at Off the Record this week," Kate said, then glanced at me. "Or maybe you didn't know since you never come to any Thursday Therapy happy hours."

"I leave all the happy hours to you."

Kate rolled her eyes. "Networking won't kill you, Annabelle."

"I network," I said. "Just not on Thursday nights." Or actually any nights since I'd started living with Reese. Tossing back cocktails with other wedding planners held significantly less appeal now that I had a hunky guy to come home to, not that I'd ever been a big fan of late night drinking with colleagues.

"Our pal Brianna doesn't have a hot cop fiancé," Kate said, as if reading my mind. "If I know her, she'll be here."

Fern made a face. "Why would you want to see that tramp? She's done nothing but spread false rumors about you and try to sabotage your business."

Technically, that was true. It was also true that Fern had done his bit to spread competing rumors about Brianna, telling anyone who'd listen that she was really a madam running a call girl business instead of planning weddings. Brianna hadn't been pleased.

"She might know something about Brock McCoy." Kate reclined back onto the seat, wedging herself between the two of us. "At the very least, we can make her twitch for a while."

"Why do I have the feeling this is more about torturing Brianna than helping our bride?" I asked.

"Annabelle." Kate pressed a hand to her chest, which was practically bare in her low-cut top. "You wound me. The thought that I would put a personal vendetta above the needs of our dear —"

"Okay, okay." I waved a hand to quiet her. "That's pouring it on a little thick, don't you think?"

She gave me her sweetest smile. "You call this a personal vendetta. I call it entertainment."

The White House came into view on our right, and the driver made a sharp left then another to swing up into the circular drive fronting the historic Hay-Adams Hotel.

I hesitated as Kate nudged me to open the door. "I'm really not sure this is going to help the case."

"It will help my mood to see Brianna squirm." Kate gave me a push from behind. "Besides, didn't Miss Evangeline say a blonde was creeping around Amanda's house? Brianna is as blond as they come. In every sense of the word."

Bold words since Kate herself was blonde, although not naturally.

We all exited the car on the passenger side, and the car drove up and idled off to the side. The doorman I'd known for years smiled when he saw us.

"Here for dinner?" He asked when he saw our attire.

"Just a quick drink." Kate batted her eyelashes at him. "Is it okay if our Lyft waits for us for a few minutes?"

He nodded, as we hurried through the ornate wooden doors and into the lobby. There were only a handful of guests sitting in burgundy upholstered armchairs in clusters to each side of the door.

We walked through the small lobby, ducking down a short hallway to the left to an unobtrusive door tucked in a corner. Kate opened it, and we started down the winding staircase that led to the basement bar.

"I'm glad we're doing this at the beginning of the evening and not the end," Fern said from behind me.

I knew what he meant. Circular stairs would not be so easy after a few drinks.

At the bottom of the stairs, we entered the subterranean bar with crimson walls, polished hardwood floors topped with Persian carpets, tufted red banquettes, and a bar with red-and-black roll-back stools. Even though it was still light outside, Off the Record was lit by small shaded lamps on cocktail tables and the warm glow of brass chandeliers.

Since it was still early in the evening, the place wasn't packed, and it was easy to find the group of wedding planners clustered at the bar.

"There she is," Kate whispered, nodding her head toward the leggy blonde holding a martini glass and laughing.

"Are you sure about—?" I started to ask, but Kate had already started making her way over to the group.

Fern grabbed my arm and propelled me forward. "Let's go. We're her backup."

I wasn't sure how intimidating Fern and I were as backup since I was in a cocktail dress and he was wearing a black silk jacquard suit that looked like it would pop a seam if he moved too quickly. The only thing slightly dangerous about the two of us was the jeweled stick pin holding his celadon-green ascot in place.

"Oh, look," Brianna said when Fern and I walked up to where she and Kate appeared to be facing off, her eyes flitting to us and then away. "More of you."

"Good to see you out and about, Brianna." Fern let his gaze drift over the women around her. "Some of your girls, I assume."

Brianna bristled noticeably, her jaw tightening. "I don't know what you're implying—"

"Me?" Fern let out a peal of laughter. "I'm not implying a thing." He winked at her. "You know I would never judge, sweetie."

Her eyes narrowed, but before she could snap back, Kate held up her hands.

"We're not here to pick a fight. We just wanted to pop by for a quick drink."

One of the other planners smiled at us. "Their martinis are on special for the next thirty minutes. We're trying to drink as many as we can."

I could feel Fern perk up next to me, but I put a hand on his arm. If we started drinking here, we might never leave, and no way was I spending my bachelorette party hanging out with my wedding planner nemesis.

"Sounds great," Kate said, not making a move to order. She turned her gaze back to Brianna. "I'm surprised to see you here, considering."

"Considering what?" Brianna's lip curled up.

"Well, isn't your boyfriend missing?" Kate smiled sweetly at her. "It's been all over the news."

"I don't have a boyfriend."

The women around Brianna shot her confused looks and began to whisper behind her.

"That's not what we heard," Kate said. "We heard that you and Brock McCoy were pretty tight."

The blonde's eyes flashed. "Who told you that? We were only friends. His wife made sure of that." As soon as she spit out the words, her eyes widened, and she sucked in a quick breath.

Kate glanced quickly at me.

"What do you mean?" I asked before Kate could continue. "His wife knew about you throwing yourself at him?"

"I didn't," she sputtered, then clamped her mouth shut. "I don't have to talk to you. My relationship with Brock is none of your business."

"Maybe not." Kate shrugged. "But her cop fiancé who's leading the case into the guy's disappearance might think it's his business. Right, Annabelle?"

I pulled my phone out of my purse. "That's right."

"Fine." Brianna shot daggers at me. "Brock and I went out to lunch a few times after I appeared on the morning show for Wedding Week. But nothing happened between us. I swear."

"Because his wife found out and stopped it?" Kate asked.

Brianna folded her arms across her chest. "Because that crazy woman threatened me and keyed my car."

Kate and I exchanged a glance. Amanda could be intense and a little spoiled, but I couldn't imagine her vandalizing someone's car. Then again, I'd never seen her react to her husband potentially cheating on her.

"And you're sure you didn't have an affair with him?" Kate eyed her as if she didn't believe the woman's story. "Why would his wife key your car over lunch?"

"I'm positive. And it ended way before he disappeared, so

you can forget about me having any reason to be involved with that." Brianna shifted from one foot to the other. "But it wasn't his wife who keyed my car."

"I thought you said—?" I started to say.

"I said that crazy woman keyed my car. His publicist." Brianna flipped her bouncy blond curls off her shoulder. "I got the feeling I wasn't the first woman his publicist had dealt with, though. To be honest, I was glad it ended when it did. That guy is a player and his publicist is a nightmare."

I studied Brianna's face, but she didn't appear to be lying. And I had to agree with her on both accounts.

CHAPTER 25

"Do you believe her?" Kate asked me, raising her voice to be heard over the thumping music.

"Strangely, I do," I yelled back. "What I don't believe is *this*."

I swiveled my head to take in the dimly lit nightclub Fern had brought us to. The space itself wasn't notable—exposed brick walls, a long bar running along one side, and a huge mirror hanging between flat screen TVs across from it. It smelled like a typical club, too—stale beer and a cacophony of aftershaves and colognes. What was notable were the hundreds of shirtless men surrounding us.

"Isn't it great?" Fern grinned widely as he surveyed the scene. "Shirtless men drink free on Thursdays."

"Interesting choice for a bachelorette party." Kate frowned as she assessed the men, quickly determining that none of them were looking at us.

"It's perfect for a bachelorette," Fern said, cupping a hand around his mouth so we could hear him over the din of chatter and the throbbing base of the music. "I knew the handsome detective wouldn't want us going anyplace where his bride-to-be would be ogled. This way, we can enjoy ourselves without you two getting hit on all night."

"Hooray," Kate deadpanned.

"My thoughts exactly," Fern said, not picking up on her sarcasm or not caring. "The real fun starts at midnight when it becomes men in underwear drink free."

Kate's face looked stricken. "This is like being at one of those all-you-can-eat Argentinian meat carving restaurants and being a vegetarian."

Fern motioned to the bar with his head. "I'll get us drinks." He disappeared into the crowd, although it was easy to follow his progress through the crowd since he was one of the few non-barechested people in the place.

"This isn't exactly what I had in mind." Kate gave me an apologetic look. "I probably shouldn't have let Fern have free rein."

"It's fine. He's right." I shouted close to her ear. "No one's hitting on us."

A man with what I could have sworn was an oiled chest sidled by me, giving me a quick once-over. "Fabulous dress, sweetie."

"Thanks," I said, wondering if Reese would have really preferred this to us going to a regular bar. "At least we learned some new information about Brock."

"I don't know what to think about the guy anymore," Kate admitted. "He's only been married for six months and it sounds like his flirtation with Brianna happened at least a month or two ago. And if she wasn't the first one, that doesn't look great for him."

"It gives us more people who might have wanted to make him disappear. Especially if he was involved with women who were married, like him."

Kate's eyes grew round. "You're right. We haven't considered the jealous husband angle. If my wife was screwing around with a guy as hot as Brock McCoy, I might want to remove him from the picture. That means he could have been offed by a spurned lover or a jealous husband."

"We don't know he was offed for sure," I reminded her.

"They found that armband with blood, right?" Kate asked. "And it was his blood, right?"

"Well, yeah."

Kate nodded her head slowly. "Oh, he's dead all right."

I swallowed hard, suspecting my assistant might be right. Things weren't looking good for our former groom, especially the more we learned about him.

Fern reappeared balancing three highball glasses in his hands. Behind him were Buster and Mack, each with a drink in hand. Luckily, they were wearing their usual leather. I wasn't sure if I could handle my burly florists shirtless.

"You made it!" Kate cried when she saw them.

"We've been here a while." Mack glanced around him. "It took a while to find you."

Kate winked at him. "We're the only ones in shirts."

"I see that now," he said.

Although our Christian biker duo wouldn't look out of place at a biker bar, they didn't exactly blend here. But they were getting plenty of stares. If you didn't look closely at the patches on their leather vests to see that their MC club was the "Road Riders for Jesus," they could appear pretty menacing. Another reason we wouldn't need to worry about unwanted attention.

"You left Merry with Prue?" I asked Buster as he sidled up next to me. He and Mack rarely ventured out after-hours, mostly because of Merry.

"They're both probably in bed by now." Buster looked like he might rather be in bed than in a loud nightclub with sweaty, shirtless men.

A heavily tattooed man passed us, and Mack's mouth fell open. "Cheese and crackers! I think he goes to our church, but I've never seen him at Biker Baptist so casually dressed."

Fern handed me one of the drinks he was balancing. "They

aren't known for their craft cocktails here, so I got us gin and tonics. You can't mess up a G and T."

I took my cocktail and started to drink, but Fern held out a hand to stop me.

"We have to toast," he said, lifting his glass high. "To a beautiful bride and wonderful wedding planner."

My face warmed, although it could have been the crowd pressing in on me. "Thanks, Fern." I clinked my glass with his, Kate's, Buster's and Mack's and took a swig. As I swallowed, I thought he might have been wrong about bad gin and tonics being impossible to make. It felt like my drink was almost all gin, and not the good stuff.

Kate grimaced. "This is definitely not a craft cocktail."

"Well, I don't care what it is," Richard said as he joined us. "I need a drink of something."

I stared at him. "I thought you were at Reese's bachelor party."

He snatched my drink and took a long swallow, then handed it back to me. "I was. Have you ever attended a bachelor party, darling?"

Not shockingly, I hadn't.

He didn't wait for me to answer. "There's only so much beer drinking and sports watching I can take in one sitting. I am officially full up for the rest of the year. Or perhaps my lifetime."

"That's all they're doing?" I asked, secretly pleased my fiancé wasn't at a strip club.

Richard nodded. "Why they call the place Church Hall is beyond me. I've never seen a church hall look like that before."

"The bachelor party is at a church hall?' Mack locked eyes with Buster. "Maybe we should have gone to that party."

"Not that kind of church hall," I said. Church Hall was an underground Georgetown sports bar. I didn't know much about it, but I knew it was pretty tame compared to some of the gentleman's clubs in the city. Or the Green Lantern, where we were.

Richard seemed to notice his surroundings for the first time since walking up to us. He twisted his head, then his eyebrows shot heavenward. "Did they confiscate everyone's shirts around here?"

"Shirtless men drink free on Thursdays," Fern told him with a grin. "Fancy a free drink?"

"If you think I'm taking off my Armani jacket in this place you're out of your mind." Richard smoothed the front of his charcoal gray blazer. "And don't even think of saying the words 'coat check' to me. I refuse to sacrifice any more clothing to the coat check gods."

"Don't worry," I said. "None of us are shirt-free."

Richard cast his eyes around our group. "Thank heavens for small favors."

I ignored his barb and decided it wasn't meant for me. I leaned in close to Richard so he could hear me. "So, is Reese having as much fun as we are?"

"Since he loves beer and sports, I'd hazard to say he's having more." Richard crossed his arms over his chest. "Why are we not at a restaurant right now?"

"It's a bachelorette party," Fern said.

Richard narrowed his eyes at him. "Is it?"

I took another sip of my drink, wincing at the high gin content. "We popped into Off the Record before we came here."

"Why on earth did you leave?" Richard shot daggers at a sweaty, shirtless man who bumped into him.

"It's Therapy Thursday," Kate told him. "The place is crawling with wedding planners."

Richard wrinkled his nose. "I'm not sure which is worse, but at least wedding planners won't sweat all over my Egyptian cotton."

"Fine." Fern let out a tortured sigh. "We'll finish our drinks and head to the next bar."

"I'm picking the next bar." Richard took my drink from me again and nearly drained it. "Let's go."

I set my not-quite-empty glass on a nearby hightop table and turned toward the exit. Luckily, Buster and Mack took the lead, pushing through the crowd like they were parting the Red Sea. Behind them, Richard held his arms wide so the crush of barechested men couldn't fill the wake, and I kept close to his heels with Kate and Fern behind me. Our single file procession snaked down a flight of stairs and outside to the sidewalk.

"Our Lyft is two minutes out." Kate held up her phone as we walked a few steps from the doors of the yellow stucco building.

"I'm guessing Reese didn't mind you taking off early?" I asked Richard, glad I didn't have to yell anymore but not happy my ears were ringing.

"I told him I was going to come keep an eye on you, so he was very supportive." Richard winked at me. "That man has got a bit of an overprotective streak, you know."

"I know."

"Of course, he wasn't too worried when I told him you were at The Green Lantern."

I could just imagine Reese's reaction when he'd heard where I was. Even though I couldn't see the smirk on his face, it still made me want to smack him.

"He wouldn't be worried," Fern said. "He knows you're with us."

"That's right," Mack added, his voice a low rumble.

I suspected he wasn't worried because I was out clubbing at gay bars, although Buster and Mack were impressive defenders if I needed them.

"Then he got a call from work, and he and his brother started talking shop."

"Daniel?" Kate's head swung toward us.

"Was it about the McCoy case?" I asked.

Richard shrugged. "Something about the cell phone records they'd finally gotten. Your husband-to-be seemed shocked that one name had popped up over and over."

"Do you remember the name?"

Richard tapped a finger to his chin. "You know I would never eavesdrop, darling, and the bar was pretty loud."

I crossed my arms in front of me, drumming my fingers on them. "Richard."

"Fine." He sighed. "But if I tell you, you have to promise me that you won't obsess about it and completely forget that we're supposed to be out celebrating your last days as a single woman."

"I promise."

"You're a horrible liar," Richard said, touching a hand to his perfectly coifed hair. "But I know you won't stop hounding me until I tell you. Or worse, you'll insist we go back to that macho bar, and you'll hound your poor fiancé."

"He's not wrong," Kate said under her breath.

I continued to stare down Richard.

"Ava," he finally said with a burst of breath. "The person Brock McCoy called the most was named Ava."

CHAPTER 26

"$\mathcal{I}$ can't believe he didn't answer my calls." I looked down at my phone as Kate and I walked up the stairs to my apartment later that night, my hand clutching the bannister tightly for support.

Kate's strappy sandals were hooked over one finger as she carried them up, so her feet padded quietly on the cold floor. "I doubt he could hear his phone ringing in a sports bar."

I knew she was right, but it still irked me that my fiancé hadn't answered my calls. Part of me thought that he was avoiding me. He probably suspected I was calling about the tidbit of information Richard shared with me. Of course, he would have been right.

"What do you think Brock's calls to his sister-in-law mean?" I asked Kate once we'd reached the landing outside my apartment door.

"The same thing I thought it meant an hour ago." Kate leaned against the wall and sighed. "Something was going on between them." She sniffed the air. "Do you smell pizza?"

I gave a brusque shake of my head, although I did smell pizza. "With his wife's sister? No way."

"Why not? She's pretty stunning." Kate put a hand to her stomach. "I would kill for a slice of pizza right now."

I dug in my purse for my keys. "That's beside the point. He obviously had plenty of opportunity to meet other women and even get chased by other women."

"Brianna," Kate added.

"Exactly." I found my key and focused on getting it in the keyhole, not wanting to admit that I was a little tipsier than I'd thought I was or that the scent of pizza had my stomach rumbling. "He could have had any woman. Why would he have an affair with his wife's sister? That seems pretty heartless on both of their parts."

"Especially since Amanda and Ava are so close." Kate straightened up. "Maybe they were planning some sort of surprise party for Amanda. That would explain all the calls."

I tilted my head at her. "But an affair would explain why Ava's husband would have been extorting Brock. If he found out, he could have held that over both of their heads."

Kate nodded slowly. "That would explain a lot that my surprise party theory doesn't."

I paused with my key in the door. "But it doesn't explain his disappearance. If you were trying for a big pay day, you wouldn't hurt the guy, right? If he's gone, he can't exactly pay up."

"Do you think Brock's publicist knew about Ava?" Kate asked. "She seemed to be pretty aggressive in handling other flirtations."

I shrugged. "It seems unlikely she didn't know about the extortion. It sounds like more than one person knew about the fight at the station."

"Knowing how tough she is, I'm surprised Darren Spencer isn't the one who disappeared." Kate touched a hand to her temples. "Is it me or are we talking in circles?"

I pushed open the door, stopping on the threshold.

"Daniel!" Kate pushed past me, her eyes going from my fiancé and his brother sprawled on the couch to the box open between them. "Pizza!"

"You're home," I said, dropping my purse to the floor.

Reese sat up and grinned at me. "I was waiting for you."

The irritation I'd felt at him for not picking up my calls evaporated as I looked into his hazel eyes. "You got pizza."

He glanced toward the unopened box on the coffee table. "I got a sausage and green pepper just for you."

"Really?" The rumbling in my stomach grew louder, and I eyed the box greedily.

"Is this pepperoni?" Kate sat on Daniel's lap and reached for one of the last pieces in the open pizza box.

I tried not to stare at Kate as she sat on my fiancé's older brother's lap. She'd always enjoyed flirting with him and had planted a few very public kisses on the guy. Who could blame her? He had the same dark good looks as Reese with just a hint of gray hair at his temples. And after a few cocktails, I suppose I should be grateful she wasn't making out with him.

Reese patted his own lap, grinning wickedly at me. "Aren't you going to tell me about your wild bachelorette party?"

I sat on his lap but narrowed my eyes at him. "Why? What do you know?"

He shrugged, the edges of his mouth twitching as if he was trying not to laugh. "Just that Richard said he was going to meet you at The Green Lantern."

I attempted to give him a stern look. "And I suppose you know all about The Green Lantern?"

Reese lost his battle not to smile, a wide grin splitting his face. "And their Shirtless Thursdays."

I swatted at him. "I'll bet you're loving this."

"A little bit," he admitted, wrapping his arms around me and pulling me into him. "More than I would have liked you at a regular bar being hit on by creepy guys."

"Well, no one hit on us at The Green Lantern."

"It was strange," Kate said after swallowing a bite of pizza. "I'm used to getting way more free drinks."

Daniel chuckled and shifted Kate on his lap. "I'm sure you are."

I swiveled my gaze back to my fiancé. "You didn't happen to suggest it to Fern, did you?"

He held his palms up. "I promise I had nothing to do with it, although I do need to remember to thank Fern."

I rolled my eyes. "This is turning out to be a seriously weird wedding week."

"If it makes you feel better, Annabelle," Daniel said. "Our night was pretty tame."

Kate cocked her head at him. "No strip clubs?"

"Not really our deal," Daniel said. "After working vice when I was a cop, I could never go back to those places."

I'd never asked Daniel about his years as a cop, but I knew he'd also risen to be a detective before retiring and starting his own private security firm. A firm we'd used on more than one occasion.

"So, sports, beer, and pizza?" I asked, glancing at the game on the flat screen that they'd muted when we came in.

Reese nodded. "A perfect night." He rubbed a hand down my bare leg. "Well, perfect now that you're here."

"You're good," I told him, brushing his one errant curl off his forehead. "I may have to marry you."

He wiggled his eyebrows. "I may have to let you."

Kate jumped up, pulling Daniel with her. "And that's our cue to leave."

"Don't you want your clothes?" I asked, since Kate had changed from her daytime outfit earlier and left her discarded clothes in my bedroom.

She shook her head, but grabbed the pizza box with the remaining slice of pepperoni. "I'll get them tomorrow." She glanced at Daniel. "You can drive me home, right?"

His gaze went to the empty beer bottles on the coffee table. "How about I grab us a cab?"

She smiled at him and held up her phone. "I think you mean a Lyft, boomer."

"See you tomorrow, bro," Daniel said as Kate tugged him out of the apartment, and the door shut with a heavy thud.

"Alone at last." Reese pulled me closer and nuzzled my neck. "I've been hanging out with guys all night long. You smell good enough to eat."

A jolt went through me as his words buzzed my earlobe, but I tried to ignore the flutter of my pulse. "Not so fast, buddy. Why didn't you answer my calls?"

He leaned back, his expression perplexed. "Your calls?"

I nodded. "I called you a bunch of times after Richard told me about Ava."

He blew out a breath. "I thought he'd overheard me. Your friend is pretty sneaky, by the way."

"He's your friend now, too." I leaned forward and opened the pizza box on the coffee table, the aroma of sausage and green pepper wafting up as I picked out a gooey slice.

"You knew him first."

I took a bite, savoring the melted cheese and spicy sausage as I chewed. It was almost funny that we were arguing about who held claim to Richard, although I knew that as much as he'd grown to like Reese, Richard was still my best friend.

"So, is it true?" I asked after I'd swallowed. "Did Brock McCoy really call his sister-in-law a lot?"

Another deep sigh. "Yes, but we don't know that it means anything yet."

I gave him a skeptical look. "Why would those two be talking so much?"

He twitched one shoulder up. "There could be reasons."

"What would you think if you found out I was talking to Daniel that much?" I took another bite, crunching into a sliver of green pepper.

His brows furrowed. "That would be weird. Why would you need to talk to my brother?"

"Exactly my point," I said, dabbing at my lips. "Unless they were planning some crazy surprise party for Amanda, there's not much reason for them to talk so much."

"A surprise party?"

"Kate's suggestion."

"Well, if they were planning a party, it's going to be something impressive because they've been calling each other for months. Sometimes multiple times a day."

So probably not a party, I thought. I still hated the idea of Amanda's sister messing around with her husband. "It does explain why a blonde would have been creeping around their house and maybe why the brother-in-law was trying to black-mail Brock."

"The sister and brother-in-law are looking pretty wrapped up in this," Reese said, then took my half-eaten pizza and put it back in the box. "But right now, that's not either of our concern."

"Hey!" I said as he stood up, picking me up at the same time. "What are you doing?"

He started walking toward our bedroom, chucking low. "For someone as clever as you are, Miss Archer, I would think you'd have figured that out by now."

CHAPTER 27

"You have to go in to work?" I asked Reese the next morning as we stood in our kitchen. I wore one of his oversized T-shirts as a nightshirt, and he was already in khakis and a button-down with the sleeves rolled up.

"We're bringing Ava and her husband in for questioning."

I almost dropped my bottled mocha Frappuccino. "You didn't tell me that last night."

He closed the distance between us, putting a hand on my waist. "I had other things on my mind last night."

My cheeks warmed even as I tried to maintain my indignant outrage. "Are you arresting them?"

"Not yet. We don't have much evidence, so we need to question them and hope one of them breaks." He grabbed his toast as it popped up in the toaster. "We still don't know where Brock McCoy is or what happened to him."

I knew it was frustrating to my fiancé to be working a potential murder case with no body. Technically, it was still a missing persons case, but I got the feeling he didn't hold out much hope that Brock was okay.

"Don't worry, babe." He kissed me softly then took a bite

of toast. "I'll be back in plenty of time to get changed for our rehearsal dinner."

I'd almost forgotten about the dinner, and for a moment, I didn't remember where Kate had been able to book at the last minute.

He must have noticed my expression because he laughed. "It's at The Iron Gate Inn."

"Right." Now it rushed back to me. Not everyone was willing to be outside in July, so Kate had managed to get us space in the grapevine covered courtyard. The Mediterranean restaurant was candlelit and romantic, so I knew even my mother would approve.

"I haven't seen your usual wedding day timeline lying around, so don't forget that Daniel is picking up your father from the airport, and I'm staying with him tonight."

I rubbed my head, thinking I might need some aspirin. "You're staying with my father?"

"No." He laughed. "I'm staying at my brother's place."

"What?" If he'd mentioned this, I'd definitely forgotten it in all the chaos. "I mean, that's great of your brother to pick up my dad, but why are you staying with him tonight?"

He shrugged. "Richard's orders. Apparently, he's staying here tonight so we don't bring any bad luck on ourselves by seeing each other before the wedding."

I fought not to roll my eyes. It always surprised me when Richard whipped out a superstition, but after I'd seen his collection of tiny voodoo dolls, I'd stopped questioning his beliefs. No way did I want to get a needle through a vital organ. "This should make for an interesting night."

Reese grinned. "Better you than me, babe." He backed toward the door. "I'm guessing this place is going to get pretty busy later on."

I glanced down at the T-shirt that barely reached mid-thigh. "Kate's swinging by the dry cleaner to pick up my rehearsal dinner dress and hers, and Fern wanted to do my hair for tonight, but aside from that, I don't have much on my plate today."

"Yet."

He had a point. My days had a way of picking up speed, especially days before weddings.

"We're here!"

Reese tilted his head at me as the warbly voice drifted to us from the front door. "See?"

I hated how right he was. He disappeared from the kitchen, and I poked my head over the divider between the two rooms, my mouth dropping open when I saw Leatrice, my mother and Fern bustling past Reese to get into my apartment.

I darted another glance to my bare legs and groaned. Just great.

"What are you doing here?" I called out, my gaze locking on Fern's as he carried a pair of tote bags past me and set them on my dining room table. "I didn't think we needed to start getting ready until the afternoon."

"We thought we'd make a spa day of it, sweetie." Fern gave me a knowing look. "I'm guessing you haven't done your nails yet, am I right?"

He was, but I didn't want to admit it. "So, you're going to be here all day?"

"Won't it be fun?" Leatrice clapped her hands as she bounded into the living room, her hot-pink ruffled dress jingling as she moved. It wouldn't be her first dress with bells sewn into the skirt, but I hoped she'd chosen a jingle-free dress for my wedding.

"Are you just waking up, Annabelle?" My mother asked, setting her purse on the couch and making a face at the beer bottles still sitting on the coffee table. "I see you had a late night."

"That wasn't me," I said. "Ree . . . Michael and his brother were hanging out last night."

She nodded but wrinkled her nose.

Before anyone could come into the kitchen, I scooped my phone from the counter and dashed down the hall, dialing Kate as I went.

"Hey, boss," Kate said when she answered. "What's up?"

Kate sounded surprisingly chipper. She also sounded like she was in her car.

"Are you on your way to the dry cleaner?" I asked, ducking into my bedroom and closing the door.

"Just left my place."

I let out a relived breath. "Great. I need you to pick me up."

"To go to the dry cleaner? I thought the whole point of me picking up your dress was so you didn't have to? You know, you're not very good at the whole 'being a bride' thing."

I lowered my voice even though the door was closed, and I could only hear muffled voices through it. "Fern showed up with Leatrice and my mother. Apparently, we're doing a whole spa day."

"Say no more. Meet me outside in ten."

I hung up and tossed the phone on my unmade bed as I took off Reese's T-shirt and rummaged through my closet for a dress to throw on. Once I'd found a blue shirtwaist dress that was both clean and unwrinkled, I buttoned it up and stepped into a pair of black flats. I popped into the bathroom on the hallway just long enough to brush my hair into a ponytail, swipe on a tinted moisturizer, and give my lashes a coat of mascara.

"Where are you going?" Fern asked when I reappeared in the living room, grabbing my purse from the floor and dropping my phone inside.

"Just a quick errand," I said, noticing that Leatrice and my mother were already reclining on my couch and Fern was standing behind them applying some sort of purple clay to their faces. "I'll be back before you can miss me."

I didn't wait for a reply, dashing out the door and down the stairs. Only when I was standing outside my building did I release a breath.

"Get in!" Kate yelled from her open window as her car screeched to a stop in front of me.

I ran in front of her car and jumped in the passenger side, barely getting the door closed before she peeled off. "You don't have to drive so fast. I'm pretty sure Fern isn't going to chase me on foot."

Kate glanced over as she careened around a corner. "But Leatrice might."

I clutched the door handle as we bounced across Wisconsin Avenue, closing my eyes as Kate swerved into a partial space in front of the dry cleaners.

"So, what's the plan after this?" she asked, opening her door.

I craned my neck to check for traffic before I opened my side. "I hadn't thought past getting out of my apartment." I joined Kate on the sidewalk. "A full day getting beauty treatments seemed like a lot."

"I feel that," Kate said. "The last time Fern set up shop in your living room, Leatrice came out looking like a very weathered Marilyn Monroe."

We walked into the small dry cleaning shop, the bell over the glass door tinkling to announce our arrival. As always, the air in the shop held the scent of chemicals.

"We can always go for breakfast at Patisserie Poupon." Kate nudged me. "It's been ages since we've had chocolate croissants."

A woman with short dark hair emerged from the back of the shop, her face breaking into a smile when she saw us.

"Archer," she said, pressing a button before I could answer. The rotating clothes rack behind her began to move the plastic covered garments hanging from the ceiling, the gears grinding.

My eyes caught on a flash of a logo as it passed. "Can you stop the machine?"

The woman stopped it, her brows pressed together in confusion. "You see your dress?"

"No." I clutched Kate's arm. "But is that a USC T-shirt?"

CHAPTER 28

"I can't believe you took someone else's clothes," Kate said as we walked out of the dry cleaners, each holding clothes encased in clear plastic.

"I didn't *take* them."

Kate's eyebrows rose dangerously high, and she stared at the wire hanger hooked over my finger. "What would you call walking out with clothes that clearly aren't yours?"

"Borrowing," I said, heading for her car.

"You're just lucky the lady remembered us picking up stuff for Amanda and Brock during their wedding." Kate pressed her car toggle and the doors automatically opened.

"I think she may be under the misconception that we're some sort of personal assistant."

"Because that's what you implied," Kate reminded me.

I got in the passenger side and put the clothes in the back. "Well, it worked didn't it?"

Kate plopped down next to me. "I still don't understand why we have some of Brock's clothes."

"It's his USC shirt. Don't you remember that Miss Evangeline said he always wore his USC shirt to run?"

"That doesn't mean it's this shirt," Kate said turning on the car and blasting the AC. "Besides, why would the shirt he left the house in that morning be at the dry cleaner?"

"An excellent question. A T-shirt isn't normally something you dry clean. Neither are running tights, but both are in the bag." Before I could continue, my phone trilled loudly. I fished it out of my purse and looked at the screen. "It's Richard." I answered and put the phone to my ear. "Hey, I—"

"Where are you?"

I heard voices in the background and lots of giggling. "Where are *you*?"

"Your apartment," he said. "Where you're supposed to be."

"Sorry. I had to run out when…"

"You don't have to tell me why you left." Hermès yipped in the background. "It's not pretty over here. Lots of purple mud and bare feet."

"Well, we aren't too far away, but I'm not sure when I'm coming back."

"Then tell me where you are, and I'll come to you." A door slammed and then there was the sound of rapid footsteps.

"We were actually headed over to our bride's house."

Richard let out a sigh. "This again. Fine. I'll meet you there. Anything is better than spa day with Leatrice. Fern's doing his best, but there is no way to combat that many wrinkles. By the way, he might be giving your mother highlights."

"Great." I rubbed a hand across my forehead. "As long as those aren't purple."

Richard signed off, as I heard him get in his car.

"So, we're going to see Amanda, and Richard is joining us?" Kate asked as she jerked her car out into the street.

I nodded, speed dialing Reese. After a few rings, it went to voicemail. I told him what we'd found and where we were going before hanging up and dropping my phone back in my purse. "He must still be interviewing Ava and her husband."

Kate shook her head as the car began bouncing on the cobbled stones of the historic street. "For a bride and groom getting married this weekend, you two sure are busy with things that have nothing to do with your wedding."

"A lot of couples stay busy right up to their wedding day. Remember Joel?"

Kate shot me a look. "He was the assistant chief of staff at the White House. I'd say his job was a little more essential than ours."

"Hey," I said. "For a bride on her wedding weekend, no one is more essential than us."

Kate muttered something about delusions of grandeur as she pulled into a driveway a few doors down from Amanda's townhouse. I heard a sharp car horn behind us and twisted my neck around to see Richard pulling in behind us. Technically, we couldn't be blocking the sidewalk in Georgetown, but I had no plans to stay long. I didn't even know if Amanda would be home.

I got out of the car and was joined by Richard and Kate. Richard wore a green button-down that looked freshly pressed with his leather crossbody bag over one shoulder. Hermès poked his head out of the bag's flap and gave us a friendly yip.

"You didn't want to leave Hermès at my place?" I asked.

Richard drew in a sharp breath. "Not on your life. Who knows what kind of beauty treatment Fern would have tried on him? After that close call with him nearly giving my dog a perm, I'm not taking chances."

"I thought he only mentioned a perm once," Kate said.

"And that was as close a call as I'd like to have, thank you very much." He patted the tiny Yorkie's head gruffly. "If I can spare him the pain of having to grow out a bad perm, I will."

I couldn't fault him there.

"So, we're here to console the bride because her husband is still missing?" Richard asked as we walked down the brick sidewalk toward the yellow house.

"Not exactly." I paused in front of the house and looked up.

"Annabelle has some questions for Amanda, but she hasn't shared them with me," Kate said.

Richard put a hand on my arm. "Are you investigating on your wedding rehearsal day?"

"Wedding rehearsal day isn't a thing," I said. "And I only want to ask her about Brianna and try to figure out how much she knew about Ava. Besides, it's this or spa day with Leatrice."

Richard bit the corner of his lip, the agony showing on his face. "It's like I'm living out Sophie's Choice."

"Yes," Kate drawled. "It's exactly like that." She turned her gaze to me. "We could always forget this and go get chocolate croissants."

"Why didn't you list that as one of our options?" Richard asked. "Let's go do that."

My phone rang, and I let out an impatient breath, feeling slightly better when I saw that it was Reese returning my call.

"Hey," I said. "You got my message? I assumed you were busy interviewing Ava and her husband. How did it go?"

"It didn't. At least the interview with Ava didn't."

"What does that mean?"

"She's missing. Her husband claims not to have seen her since yesterday and says some of her clothes are missing."

My mouth went dry. "She's gone?"

Both Kate and Richard gaped at me.

"Did her husband have anything else to say?" I asked my fiancé. "Anything that might shed light on what's really going on?"

"He admitted he knew his wife had an affair with Brock, but he says she ended it. Your guess was right. That was why he was blackmailing his brother-in-law. If Brock paid him off, he wouldn't tell Amanda."

"And did he?" I asked. "Pay him off?"

"He claims no, but he also swears he didn't tell his sister-in-law."

I tapped my chin. "But now both his wife and the man she screwed around with on him are missing?"

"He definitely has the best motive for any foul play, but now I'm not so sure anything happened to Brock in the first place," Reese said. "Of course, we're holding him while we search his apartment. And putting out an APB on Ava."

"You think there's a chance this was an all elaborate ruse for Brock and Ava to run off together?"

"Crazier things have happened." He paused. "Gotta run, babe. I'll see you soon."

"So, who's going to tell Amanda that her husband might have run away with her sister?" Kate I asked, then immediately raised her hand. "Not me."

"I'd rather tell her he's dead," Richard muttered.

I had a feeling he was right.

CHAPTER 29

*A*manda opened the door, appearing startled for a moment before smiling. She wore yoga pants and a Lululemon yoga top with her brown hair pulled into a messy bun. "Hey, Annabelle! Kate." Her gaze slid to Richard. "And Richard Gerard? What are you all doing here?"

"You haven't heard?" Kate asked.

I elbowed her but didn't glance over. "We thought you might need a little moral support."

She stepped back and waved us in. "I expected Ava to be here by now. She's been coming over every morning, but I guess she's running late."

We walked inside. The living room was considerably neater than it had been on Monday, and I noticed only one coffee cup on the end table next to the couch.

Richard patted Hermès, who was squirming in his leather bag, as he took a seat in an armchair. Kate and I sat on one end of the couch while Amanda took the other.

"Is that a Yorkie?" Amanda's face brightened. "I love dogs. We can't have any because of Brock's allergies, but I've been looking into some of the doodle mixes."

Richard smiled. "Hermès is a purebred Yorkie."

"If you want to let him out of your bag, I don't mind."

Amanda managed a shaky smile. "Brock isn't around to go into a sneezing fit."

Richard lifted Hermès from this bag and set him onto the floor. "Now behave yourself, young man."

As if he understood the words, Hermès was virtually silent as he ran around sniffing everyone's feet. Amanda ruffled his black-and-brown head when he inspected her.

"I don't suppose you've found out anything new?" Amanda asked, looking up from the tiny dog.

"Nothing the police don't know," I said.

She nodded. "It was stupid of me to think I could prevent bad publicity by keeping Brock's disappearance a secret. I guess I panicked since I know how paranoid my husband is about gossip and bad PR."

"I'm sure your husband's publicist impressed that on you."

Amanda gave an apologetic smile. "It sounds like you've met Teegan. She's pretty intense, but she's done wonders for Brock's career."

By threatening violence and keying cars, I thought. "You said that Brock usually ran in his USC T-Shirt."

"Always." Amanda bobbed her head up and down. "He had several. It was his way of keeping a bit of the West Coast with him. At least that's what he said."

"Does he like to dry clean his T-shirts?" I asked.

Amanda cocked her head at me. "He might be a bit preten-tious, but he doesn't dry clean T-shirts. Why?"

Her words sounded convincing, but that didn't explain why we'd found her husband's running clothes at the dry cleaners.

"We have a client who dry cleans his boxers," Kate said with a high laugh. "How crazy is that?"

I made a point not to look at Kate. We did not have a client who did that, but I knew she was covering for me. "Do you mind if I pop into your bathroom?"

"Sure." Amanda motioned to the stairs. "It's on the second floor. You know these historic townhouses."

I was very familiar with them since we had lots of George-town clients. There was even one Georgetown row house that was only eight feet wide with the stairs on the outside of the building because the house was too narrow for them to be on the inside.

"Thanks." I stood and headed up the wooden stairs, not knowing what I was looking for but just hoping to find a clue in the house that would explain what was going on. I was close to putting it all together, but there was something big missing.

When I reached the top of the stairs, I ignored the bath-room and ducked into the master bedroom. Brock McCoy was missing and so was Ava, and they'd been involved with each other. It seemed impossible that Amanda wouldn't have known or been involved with their disappearance. Her brother-in-law claimed not to have told her about the affair, but I suspected the wife knew. And who else would care enough to make them both disappear? Unless this really was an elaborate ruse for the pair to disappear together.

The queen-sized bed was neatly made, the mass of decora-tive pillows covering most of the snow-white duvet. Matching bedside tables flanked each side and it was easy to tell Brock's from Amanda's—his had a bookmarked thriller while hers had an oversized mug, an orange pill container, and a framed wedding photo.

My phone vibrated in my dress pocket, and I answered it quickly when I saw it was Fern. "I'm a little busy," I whispered.

"You are coming back, aren't you?" he asked. "I have a lot of work to do on you, sweetie. It's probably been months since you had a pedicure, am I right?"

"You want to give me a pedicure?"

"Of course." He sounded aghast. "As if I would send you down the aisle with Hobbit feet."

I thought "hobbit feet" was a little harsh. "I'm coming back,

I promise. We went to the dry cleaners and then popped in to say hi to Amanda."

There was silence on the other end, and I walked to the window that overlooked the front of the house.

"You're investigating?" The disapproval was thick in Fern's voice.

I pulled back the curtains and looked down onto the brick sidewalk shaded by leafy trees. From this vantage point, I had a good view of the street and of the woman striding up toward the house.

"Crap." Why hadn't I thought of it before? There was someone else who had a vested interest in making Ava disappear.

"Annabelle?" Fern's voice jerked me back to reality, and I let the curtains fall back into place.

"Sorry. I just realized something about who could be behind all this. And she just walked up to the front door."

"Anna—"

I hung up, sliding the phone back in my pocket and heading back downstairs to confront Teegan Thomas.

CHAPTER 30

"Look who happened to stop by," Kate said, as I walked back into the living room. Her smile was fixed as she looked at the blonde with the high bun.

"What are you doing here?" The publicist didn't bother to hide her displeasure at finding us. Her eyes rested on Richard. "And who is this?"

Richard put his hands on his hips and returned her glare. "Richard Gerard of Richard Gerard Catering. And who might you be?"

"I'm Teegan Thomas, the McCoy's publicist."

I noticed that she'd gone from Brock McCoy's publicist to both the McCoy's publicist.

"We stopped in to say hi to Amanda," I said. "And tell her about the latest in the case."

Something flickered behind Teegan's eyes, but her glare remained even.

"The latest?" Amanda asked, her eyes widening and going from me to Kate. "What's happened?"

"I think you should all leave," Teegan said. "I'd like to advise my client."

"I'll bet you would," Kate muttered, folding her own arms over her chest to mimic the icy blonde.

"Annabelle," Amanda said. "What's going on?"

"First of all, the police are on their way here," I lied and noticed Teegan flinch.

"Why?" Amanda's hand went to her mouth. "Is it Brock?"

"It's actually Ava," I said. "She's gone missing too."

Amanda staggered back a few feet and sank onto the couch. "My sister is missing? I don't understand."

"Maybe Teegan can explain to us," I said, focusing on the woman whose face was stone.

"Me?" She finally said, glancing around the room. "You think I had something to do with her sister being missing?"

I shrugged. "You knew she'd been having an affair with Brock, right?"

The hard press of her mouth told me I was right, but she didn't speak.

"Wait, what?" Amanda's head jerked up. "My sister and my husband?" She shook her head vigorously. "Impossible. Ava would never do that to me."

"But Brock would?" I asked, my voice softer.

She twitched one shoulder up. "Women flirted with him all the time. He might have slipped up, but never with my sister."

I looked at Teegan, who's alabaster cheeks were tinged pink. "You knew everything about Brock McCoy, didn't you? You considered it your job to keep him safe from scandal, even if it meant keying women's cars. So, when you found out about Ava, you must have swung into action."

"I might have keyed that wedding planner's car, but I have nothing to do with Ava disappearing," Teegan said, her eyes flashing.

"Oh, I think you do." I said. "And I think you also have something to do with Brock McCoy disappearing."

Her mouth gaped open, as did Amanda's.

"Teegan?" Amanda's voice cracked.

"You think I would have done anything to hurt Brock?" Her cheeks now flamed red. "I...I..."

"You loved him, didn't you?" Kate asked, her voice low.

The publicist heaved in a breath.

"I can't believe I didn't see it before." Kate shook her head slowly. "That's why you defended him so much. You genuinely hated the women he was linked with because you had a thing for him."

"I never..." Teegan said, looking at Amanda. "It wasn't like that, I promise."

"So, was it covering up for him so much that made you finally snap?" I asked. "Or was it the realization that he slept with everyone but you?"

"Fine," the woman said. "I was furious with him when I found out about Ava. I knew that this was a publicity nightmare I couldn't cover up, especially since her husband was running around threatening to expose it. I couldn't believe he'd been so stupid and reckless. After everything I'd done for him."

"So, you staged his disappearance," I said. "You made it look like he left his house to go running, but really it was you in his clothes and a knit cap. You dumped his phone on the trail then took off the clothes and dropped them at the drycleaner, which was really clever. Who would ever think to check for evidence at a dry cleaner? Those clothes would have stayed there for months. Then you returned to the house as yourself and went around the side of the house. I can only assume you had his body in the back somewhere and drove him away in your car."

Teegan shook her head.

Amanda stood. "She does have keys to the house. She used to deliver things for Brock all the time—like his dry-cleaning."

"And I'm guessing you took a sleeping pill the night before your husband vanished?" I said to Amanda with an apologetic look. "I saw the pill container on your nightstand."

She put a hand to her head. "I did. I've had a hard time sleeping lately so I take pills. They really knock me out." She swung her gaze to Teegan. "Did you kill my husband while I was upstairs sleeping?"

"I think she did," I answered before the publicist could. "I'm guessing she arrived through your back entrance knowing when Brock usually went on his run. Maybe she hadn't planned it, but I'll bet they got into an argument, and she ended up killing him in a rage or maybe accidentally. Either way, she had to cover it up. So, she pretended to be him leaving on a run, covering his armband in blood and dumping it and his phone along the trail. Then when she came back, she must have let her hair down, so she'd look like your sister. That way Ava would be implicated."

Teegan was shaking her head hard. "You can't prove any of this."

"But then something happened to make her need to get rid of Ava," Kate said. "Maybe you knew that if she testified, she'd clear herself. Or maybe you just hated her for being the catalyst for Brock's murder."

"You've got it all wrong," Teegan said.

"Offing your boss is pretty wrong," Kate said.

The publicist turned and headed for the front door. "I don't have to stand here and listen to this crap."

Before I could make a move, Amanda reached into a drawer in a side table, pulling out a black object and lunging forward. When the stun gun made contact with the publicist's back, she jerked for a second then went limp, collapsing in a heap on the ground.

We all jumped back.

"I can't believe I did that." Amanda was breathing hard as she looked down at Teegan.

"I can't believe you keep a stun gun in your living room," Richard said.

Kate took jerky steps to one of the armchairs and sat down hard. "That was crazy." She glanced up at me. "How did you figure all that out?"

"Guesses mostly. But the clothes at the dry cleaner made me realize that they'd been dropped there as a way to dispose of them, which meant they were worn over something else. It would be a safe way to get rid of them. The police might search dumpsters and trash, but not drycleaners. From there, I figured out that someone had pretended to be Brock. Luckily for Teegan, the only person looking out their window so early is an old lady with dirty windows. And she wore a knit cap and kept her head down. Then Miss Evangeline saw a blond sneaking up the side of the house later. We'd assumed it was Ava, but then I thought that maybe the real killer was setting it up to look like Ava."

"So the cops are on their way?" Richard asked.

"Not yet," I admitted. "I was bluffing about that."

"I'll call them." Amanda picked up her cell phone from the coffee table.

As she dialed, Richard glanced around the floor. "Where did Hermès go? He's usually in the middle of all the action."

I heard a whining noise coming from the back of the house. Richard must have heard it too, because he bustled off with me behind him.

We entered the bright and airy kitchen at the back of the house. It had clearly been renovated, with white subway tile on the walls and a gray and white marble island in the center. Lots of windows along the back wall overlooked a small garden in the back and a single parking spot.

"Spectacular." Richard paused for a moment when we entered, and I knew he meant the renovated kitchen and not the view.

There was a scratching noise coming from the corner, and we circled the island to see Hermès pawing at a pantry door.

"What are you doing?" Richard scooped him up. "You know it's bad manners to poke around in other people's homes."

It was hard not to notice his pointed comment. "I know, I know. But it was all to find a killer."

He rolled his eyes. "Just don't go setting a bad example for my dog, darling."

I doubted Hermès was looking to me for behavioral guidance. I was curious why he'd been so eager to get into the pantry, especially since I doubted it contained dog treats.

When Richard turned to leave, I opened the door just a crack. Something heavy inside made me leap back to avoid being hit as it knocked the door open and thudded onto the tile floor. Richard spun around and screamed as we both looked down at the very dead body of Ava Spencer.

CHAPTER 31

*K*ate ran inside the kitchen with Amanda close on her heels. We all stared down at the blonde woman, her eyes wide and lifeless.

"That's the one problem with dogs," Amanda said after several heavy moments of silence. "They get into everything."

We all swung our head to her as she opened a drawer, pulled out a gun, and leveled it at us.

"A gun in the kitchen?" Richard gaped at her. "This place is like a WASPy arsenal."

"Wait, what? You?" My head spun as I tried to digest what had just happened. "You killed your own sister?"

Amanda smiled at me. "Your theory was pretty good out there. I'm impressed by how much you got right." She made a sad face. "Aside from getting the most important detail wrong."

"So, it wasn't Teegan?" Kate asked, her voice shaky.

Amanda laughed as if we were at a garden party. "She has the persona to be a killer, doesn't she?"

Richard bobbed his head up and down.

"No," Amanda said. "You were right about one thing. She was completely in love with my husband. She never would have hurt him, as much as she hated having to watch him screw around with other women. Then again, he wasn't cheating on her. Maybe she would have felt different if she was married to him. Maybe she would have been pushed to murder if she was the one he'd promised to love and honor."

I glanced toward the living room and wondered if the woman Amanda had stunned was okay. Now I felt guilty for accusing her of so many awful things.

"So Teegan wasn't involved at all?" Kate asked. "It was all you?"

I gaped at her. "And you weren't knocked out with a sleeping pill?"

Amanda smiled. "No, although I do take them. But I didn't take them that night."

"The night after your big fight," I said.

"That's right. That part was also true. Brock and I fought outside the house and then it continued inside. I'd found out about Ava. I confronted him, thinking he would end it like he always did. I guess I hoped it was another of his flirtations or flings."

"But it wasn't," Kate said.

Amanda shook her head, her expression darkening. "He claimed to be in love with her. My own sister." She waved the gun as she talked. "Of course, Ava had always been trying to copy me. She always wanted what I had, but she rarely got it."

I remembered that Ava had only been first runner up in her pageant, a fact that Amanda had jokingly mentioned more than once on her wedding day with the other pageant queens.

"It must have been pretty upsetting to realize that she'd finally gotten something you had," I said.

Her eyes met mine, and I could see the pain in them, but also the fury. For someone who was used to being the queen bee, that must have snapped something inside of her.

"She couldn't have him. He was my husband." She jabbed a finger at her own chest. "I always win. No matter what."

"Did he tell you he was going to leave you for her?" Kate asked.

Amanda pivoted to Kate. "Can you believe that? He actually thought he was going to walk out on me after only six months. With my own sister." She gave a rough shake of her head. "It would have been a huge scandal."

"So, you killed him?" I asked, realizing that the woman had clearly snapped.

She shrugged. "I really had no choice. I thought I was being clever. I dressed up like him and left the house, dumped his phone, dropped off his clothes, and wore a wig when I snuck back in through the back door."

"A wig," Kate said in a hushed voice. "You didn't guess the wig part."

I shot her a look. "Thanks for pointing that out."

"So, Brock never left the house that day? He was already dead?"

Amanda nodded impatiently. "Cracked his skull with his broadcasting award statuette while he was in the shower. I couldn't get him out of the house without someone noticing so I had to cut him into more manageable bits I could more easily bury in the garden."

We all glanced toward the small flower garden behind the house.

Richard made a strangled sound. "I might be sick."

"Then I made one mistake," Amanda said. "I called you."

I swallowed hard as she pointed the gun at me.

"I thought it would be a perfect way to make myself look innocent. Besides, how good could a wedding planner really be at investigating crimes?" She cocked her head at me. "I was wrong about that, and I didn't know that your fiancé is a detective. Luckily, my husband had enough people who hated him that you were pretty distracted. Not to mention all the women."

I glanced down at Ava. "Why did you kill your sister?"

Amanda gazed down at the dead blonde, her hair matted with blood in the back. "I guess I couldn't let it go after all, especially when she came over every day pretending to care so much about me. She made some comment last night about what a great husband he was, and I guess I lost it."

So, the body had been shoved in her pantry since the night before. I shuddered at the thought of her sleeping with the dead body of her sister downstairs the whole time.

"Suffice it to say, you did not call the police?" Richard asked, shifting Hermès in his arms.

"No." She gave us a sad smile. "And by the time they find your bodies, I'll be long gone."

There was a noise from the front of the house, but Amanda didn't turn. "That's probably Teegan coming to. Don't worry. I tied her up, so she won't be going anywhere. I'll finish her off once I'm done here."

My mouth felt dry, and my heart hammered in my chest. Was I really going to die the day before my wedding? After I'd sent hundreds of brides down the aisle, was I really not going to get my own wedding day?

"I'm sorry, Annabelle," Amanda said. "You really were a great planner. Too bad you weren't a worse investigator."

Kate grabbed my hand and Richard moved closer to me. As Hermès started yipping, there was a flash of movement in the doorway behind Amanda, a loud pop, and then the woman dropped to the floor next to her sister.

"I got her!" my mother cried, lowering the pearl handled pistol as she stepped into the kitchen. Fern and Leatrice hurried in behind her, with Fern gasping when he saw the two women on the floor.

"Such a shame," he said, fanning himself with one hand. "They both had such good hair."

Amanda made a noise, rolling over and clutching her bleeding shoulder.

"She's not dead!" Fern cried, kicking Amanda's gun across the tile floor.

My mother looked at her gun and shrugged. "It's been a long time since I've fired this. I'm a little rusty."

I was speechless as I looked at my mother. "Mom? What are you —?" I couldn't finish the question as my throat became thick with emotion. I ran over to her and threw my arms around her. "Thanks, mom. I'm really glad you're here."

My mother gave me a squeeze. "So am I, Annabelle. It seems you got yourself in a little scrape."

"That's one way to put it," Richard muttered behind me.

"Fern said it sounded like you were in trouble again," Leatrice bounced on her toes, the tinfoil in her hair flapping. "So, we hopped in my car and rushed over. We would have been here sooner, but it was hard to find parking."

I released my mother, and she scanned the room. "Is everyone okay?"

"Everyone but those two." Kate pointed to Ava and Amanda.

There was more noise from the living room, and Reese burst into the kitchen, followed by a pair of uniformed officers.

Tears stung my eyes when I saw him, and before I could say a word he'd swept me up into a breathless hug. When he let me down, I peered up at him. "How did you know?"

"Your phone," he said, looking me up and down as if searching for injuries. "You must have butt-dialed me."

"So, you heard everything?" I asked.

He nodded, cupping my face in his hands. "Pretty much. I almost lost a year off my life when it sounded like she was going to shoot you."

"She would have," Richard said. "But luckily Gwen is handy with a revolver."

Reese looked over at my mother, who winked at him and waved her lady gun. "It's nice to see you, Michael." She motioned to Fern. "We'd better go before Leatrice's hair gets over processed."

"Actually, Gwen," my fiancé said. "You might need to come with me to the station to give a statement."

The uniformed officers pulled Amanda up from the floor as she screamed in pain. She glared at us all as they cuffed her, read her her rights, and walked her out of the kitchen.

"I'd be delighted to, Michael." My mother tucked her gun back in her purse. "Anything to corporate with the law."

"What are you doing to your hair?" Kate asked Leatrice, as she glanced at the tiny sheets of tinfoil covering the woman's head.

Leatrice beamed and shook one finger. "It's a surprise for Annabelle's wedding."

"If there is one thing Annabelle's wedding does not need any more of," Richard said, his face pale and his voice shaky, "it's surprises."

Reese pressed a kiss to my lips and tingles spread down my arms and legs. When he pulled back, he grinned down at me. "For once, I agree with Richard."

CHAPTER 32

"*I* thought I specifically said no surprises," Richard said, hands planted firmly on his hips as we stood on the second floor of the Carnegie Institute surveying the setup below.

"And this is a surprise for you?" I asked, peering over the marble railing that overlooked the rotunda.

He swung his head to me so fast I was surprised his neck didn't snap. "It's sand, Annabelle!"

"Isn't it great?" Kate walked up, already in her turquoise bridesmaid dress but wearing flip-flops instead of heels.

Richard's gaze slid to her feet then back up. "Great? One of the city's most regal buildings is being turned into a..."

"A beach," I said, as I watched Buster roll another wheelbarrow of powdery white sand into the rotunda and start to spread it over the plastic sheeting they'd laid down over the marble. A layer of the substance covered the floor, and a birch branch arch dripping with Sahara roses sat on top of it at one end. Instead of the dark heavy doors as a backdrop, my florist friends had draped layers of sheer fabric across it, and the gossamer billowed in the wind created by a pair of fans positioned to each side. The traditional gold chivari chairs my mother wanted were not there. Instead, there were rows of transparent ghost chairs. They'd even managed to hang a curtain of Sahara roses from a web of clear thread overhead, so when you looked up from floor level you saw the sand-colored roses as if they were suspended in mid-air.

"We thought you'd like it." Kate put an arm around my shoulders and looked down with me. "At least Buster and Mack and I did." She dropped her voice. "We thought it best not to tell Richard because he might be concerned about the rules and regulations."

"Of which you are breaking at least ten." Richard huffed out a breath. "I hope you don't expect Richard Gerard Catering to be liable for any damages."

"This is all Buster and Mack," Kate said to me. "They knew how disappointed you really were about having to change your wedding vision, so they did some sort of sweetheart deal with the site managers and promised to have the place cleaned from top to bottom."

A lump formed in my throat. "You didn't have to do this."

Kate bumped my hip. "Like I said, it was mostly the Mighty Morphin Flower Arrangers. And don't ask me where they found all the sand."

"I guess I didn't need the wedding shoes after all," I said, thinking of the shoe box with the scrappy sandals.

Richard sucked in a breath. "You aren't going to be barefoot all evening, are you? Only the ceremony is on sand. I *know* they aren't covering the dining room carpet with sand."

"No." I patted his arm. "I'll put on shoes for the reception, but I hope you're ready to process barefoot."

His artificially tan cheeks paled. "Me? I hadn't thought that I'd have to be barefoot."

"You are the Man of Honor," I reminded him.

"Oh, good heavens!" He bustled off, presumably to get his feet into tip-top shape.

He passed my mother, as she walked toward us in her pale pink chiffon gown. Luckily, she'd packed the dress she'd planned to wear in the Caribbean, so it fit the beach theme perfectly. She was even padding around in her bare feet.

She hesitated when she spotted me, taking in my simple chiffon gown and the fingertip length veil. "You make a beautiful bride, Annabelle."

"Thanks, mom." I wasn't used to compliments from my mother, but it seemed like this time there was no added tip on how I could look better.

"I always knew you would." She smiled at me. "You're practically glowing. Of course, that's because you're marrying that lovely boy."

I would have hardly called my tall, dark, and handsome cop a 'lovely boy,' but I didn't correct her. "I'm lucky."

She gave a brief shake of her head. "He's the lucky one." She winked at me. "Just like your father is the lucky one. Don't tell him I said that, of course." She joined us at the railing, darting a glance below. "I have to say, I like what Buster and Mack came up with."

"You do?" Kate and I said almost in unison.

She nodded. "I've learned a lot by spending time with your friends this week. Leatrice doesn't care what anyone thinks of her, which was very refreshing. And that Fern certainly marches to the beat of his own drum."

"I'm pretty sure he's got a whole marching band," Kate muttered.

My mother laughed. "Being around them showed me I could let go of some things. It was quite the revelation."

"I'm sorry I didn't get to—" I started to say, but she cut me off with a wave.

"Don't be silly. I understand. You're a busy woman with a busy job. And you were apparently tracking down a killer." She squeezed my arm. "I'm just glad you have such good friends to support you. It makes me feel better to know that you're not up here all alone."

"I've never been all alone," I said.

She nodded, and I could have sworn there were tears in her eyes. "I know that now, and I know you couldn't ask for nicer, more loyal friends. They really do love you, you know."

I looked down at Mack, shoveling sand in his leather pants and sleeveless leather vest. "I know."

She cleared her throat. "That being said, I'm getting you a small revolver to keep in your purse. Consider it a wedding present. I think in your line of work—and with brides like that one yesterday—you need it."

She gave my arm a final pat as she walked away.

"Well, it's better than another blender," Kate said. "And, to be fair, one of us probably should be packing."

"Packing?" Fern bustled up to us, his eyes large. "Who's packing?"

"Annabelle's going to start carrying a gun," Kate said.

His shoulders sagged. "I thought we were admiring delivery men or something exciting."

"Nope." I shook my head. "Just watching the set up."

"It's going to be stunning." He touched a hand to my hair that he'd already curled and sprayed to within an inch of its life in a half-up half-down style. "Of course, I would have loved it if you'd let me be a little more adventurous with your hair."

"Like you were adventurous with Leatrice?" I gave him a pointed look.

"Her hair goes perfectly with the theme of your wedding," he said.

"It's pink. She looks like Frenchy from *Grease*."

"If Frenchy had been trapped in a food dehydrator for a year," Kate said.

Fern adjusted the enormous blue topaz ring on his finger. "You know Leatrice likes to take risks. You should try it sometime."

"I cornered a killer yesterday," I said.

He sighed. "Not those kinds of risks, sweetie."

"Yoo hoo!" Leatrice's bubble gum pink head appeared at

the top of the stairs winding up from downstairs. "Can I see the bride before the wedding?"

I waved her up. "Of course."

"Can I?" Reese's deep voice made me jump.

"*You're* not supposed to see me before the wedding," I said halfheartedly as he walked up behind Leatrice with his brother a few steps behind him.

Both men were in tailored black suits with straight black ties and no shoes. Kate nudged me and made an appreciative noise in her throat, and I wasn't sure if it was about both men or just Daniel.

"I know, but things were so crazy yesterday processing your killer bride, and taking your mother's statement, then Richard still insisted on sleeping at our apartment." He crossed to me and took my hands in his. "I just needed to see you and prove to myself that you were really okay."

"I'm okay." I smiled up at him.

"You're more than okay." His eyes traveled down my dress and back to my face. "You're gorgeous."

My face warmed, and I looked him up and down at his black suit. "So are you."

"You know," Reese said. "We didn't get to practice our lines since we didn't do a rehearsal of the ceremony."

"Because someone was busy processing and booking a killer," I said.

He grinned. "Guilty."

"We can rehearse now," I said, pointing to Kate. "Kate will stand here and hold my imaginary bouquet"

"Not imaginary." Mack lumbered up, breathing heavily and holding out a handtied bouquet of Sahara roses and lush white peonies.

Buster joined him, sweat glistening on his bald head. "Your favorites."

"They are," I said, beaming at both men. "I couldn't love

anything more. Well," I glanced up at my soon-to-be husband, "Maybe one thing."

"Are we rehearsing?" Richard called out as he strode toward us in his black suit and bare feet. "Perfect. You know I hate to do anything without a run-through."

He took his place next to Reese and Daniel, and I met his eyes.

"I thought I'd get a lecture about jinxing things by seeing Reese before the ceremony," I said.

"What else could possibly happen at this point, darling? You were almost shot yesterday. Worrying about your bad luck is too much work for me. Not that it wouldn't hurt you to get your chicken bones read."

"We're not in New Orleans. Where in DC do you get your chicken bones read?" Kate asked, shuddering.

"There are places," Richard said with a quirk of his lips. "If you know the right people."

I could only imagine, but now was not the time for me to press my friend for more details.

"I'm the priest." Fern clapped his hands as he stood in front of us. "I make a very convincing priest."

My fiancé cocked an eyebrow, but didn't comment.

"Dearly beloved," Fern began in a warbly voice that sounded slightly British.

"Why don't we just go over our vows?" I whispered to him.

He shrugged. "If you want, but you're missing my favorite part."

I took Reese's hands and repeated the vows I'd heard hundreds of times in wedding ceremonies, ending with "I, Annabelle Archer, take you, Michael Reese, to be my wedded husband, to have and to hold from this day forward, for better, for worse, for richer, for poorer, in sickness and in health, to love and to cherish, till death do us part."

"Nicely done, sweetie," Fern said in a stage whisper, then nodded to my fiancé. "Now it's your turn, hot stuff."

Reese repeated the words I'd said, locking eyes with me and squeezing my hands. When he was done, he turned to Fern. "Now do we kiss?"

Fern opened his arms wide. "You may kiss the bride."

Reese swept me up into a kiss that was long enough to make Richard clear his throat. When he released me, Fern was dabbing his eyes.

"By the power vested in me by Ordination.com, I now pronounce you husband and wife."

Reese raised my hand in the air, and everyone clapped.

"I thought the ceremony was going to be downstairs," Leatrice said. "That wasn't it, was it? Did my Honeybun miss it? He has a whole Junkanoo parade planned for your recessional."

"What?" Richard spluttered. "A parade? I didn't know about this!"

"I thought Sidney Allen was keeping the entertainment low key," I said, wondering how many performers in feathered headdresses would be attending my wedding.

"You wanted an island wedding," Kate reminded me.

She was right. It would definitely feel like the Caribbean if Reese and I walked back down the aisle behind a parade of dancers in colorful, beaded costumes. "Don't worry, Leatrice. That was just the rehearsal. We won't do the real ceremony until the officiant arrives."

"But Fern is the officiant," Leatrice said.

I shook my head. "Kate booked an actual officiant." I glanced over at Kate, who looked stricken. "Didn't you?"

"Things got busy," she said, wringing her hands. "I might have forgotten."

"So, Fern is our officiant?" I twisted to look at him smiling broadly at us. "And we just got married? Like actually married?"

"I'm happy to do it again downstairs for the bigger crowd," Fern said. "But, for round two I'm definitely doing my homily."

Reese laughed and wrapped his arms around my waist. "I don't mind marrying you a second time, babe. Especially if we get a parade."

The second kiss my new husband gave me was even more pulse quickening than the first.

ALSO BY LAURA DURHAM

For Better Or Hearse

Dead Ringer

Review to a Kill

Annabelle Archer Collection: Books 1-4

To get notices whenever I release a new book, follow me on
BookBub:

https://www.bookbub.com/profile/laura-durham

This book is dedicated to Davis Richardson, who was my go-to tent guy for over twenty years, But anyone who knew Davis, knew he was so much more than a tent guy. He was a pillar in the DC event community and one of the best, kindest, and smartest people I've ever known.

Davis, you were the best of the best! The world is a little less wonderful without you in it.

xoxo

ACKNOWLEDGMENTS

As always, an enormous thank you to all of my wonderful readers, especially my beta readers and my review team. A special shout-out to the beta readers who caught my goofs this time: Patricia Joyner, Linda Reachill, Sheila Kraemer, Linda Fore, Sandra Anderson, Cathy Jaquette, Kaitlyn Platt, Carol Spayde, Annemarie Pasquale. Thank you!!

Big kisses to everyone who leaves reviews. They really make a difference, and I am grateful for every one of them!

ABOUT THE AUTHOR

Laura Durham has been writing for as long as she can remember and has been plotting murders since she began planning weddings over twenty years ago in Washington, DC. Her first novel, BETTER OFF WED, won the Agatha Award for Best First Novel.

When she isn't writing or wrangling brides, Laura loves traveling with her family, standup paddling, perfecting the perfect brownie recipe, and reading obsessively.

Find her on:
www.lauradurham.com
laura@lauradurham.com

To get notices whenever she releases a new book, follow her on BookBub:

https://www.bookbub.com/profile/laura-durham

facebook.com/authorlauradurham
instagram.com/lauradurhamauthor